# A BLOODY PREDICTION

"All right," she said. "To the future, then. As I said, I don't see marriage, I see guns . . . and I see . . . a man."

"A man?" he asked. "What man?"

She stared down at his hand for a few moments, then released it and sat back. "I'm finished."

"What? Finished? What about the man—describe him for me."

"He's a big man, dark eyes, black . . . and a black soul . . . very black . . . an evil man with whom you will clash . . . violently."

"Doesn't sound like anyone I know."

"It isn't," she said. "He's in your future."

"How far in my future?"

She hesitated, then said, "Not far."

# DON'T MISS THESE
## ALL-ACTION WESTERN SERIES
### FROM THE BERKLEY PUBLISHING GROUP

**THE GUNSMITH by J. R. Roberts**
Clint Adams was a legend among lawmen, outlaws, and ladies. They called him . . . the Gunsmith.

**LONGARM by Tabor Evans**
The popular long-running series about U.S. Deputy Marshal Long—his life, his loves, his fight for justice.

**LONE STAR by Wesley Ellis**
The blazing adventures of Jessica Starbuck and the martial arts master, Ki. Over eight million copies in print.

**SLOCUM by Jake Logan**
Today's longest-running action Western. John Slocum rides a deadly trail of hot blood and cold steel.

# THE GUNSMITH
## 155
## THE MAGICIAN

### J. R. ROBERTS

**J**
JOVE BOOKS, NEW YORK

THE MAGICIAN

A Jove Book / published by arrangement with
the author

PRINTING HISTORY
Jove edition / November 1994

ISBN: 0-515-11495-2

A JOVE BOOK®
Jove Books are published by The Berkley Publishing Group,
200 Madison Avenue, New York, New York 10016.
JOVE and the "J" design are trademarks
belonging to Jove Publications, Inc.

PRINTED IN THE UNITED STATES OF AMERICA

10  9  8  7  6  5  4  3  2  1

THE GUNSMITH
155
THE MAGICIAN

# ONE

Clint had never seen a carnival before—
and he certainly had never seen a carnival
on wheels.

Every so often he had come across a group of
traveling players or Gypsies who put on shows
to make extra money, and he had been to the
circus, but when he topped a rise just outside
of Benton's Fork, Arizona, and saw the long
line of wagons he was surprised. Most of the
wagons had writing on the side, much like
the wagons traveling salesmen used, but here
the writing was in red and it proclaimed the
dozen or so wagons to be the CARNIVAL FLORA.

The wagons were obviously in the process
of stopping and preparing to camp. Perhaps
they were even planning to set up their show
there, outside of Benton's Fork. The town was

certainly large enough to support the carnival, and people would probably come from all over the county.

Clint's original plan had been to ride right into town, but now his curiosity was up—and his gunsmithing wagon would fit right in with the carnival wagons.

He urged his team down the hill and watched the flurry of activity as he approached the camp. The activity was not due to his approach, however, but clearly a routine followed by the carnival workers as they were preparing to make camp. In fact, no one even noticed him until he was almost upon the camp, and then several people turned and spotted him. They nudged each other, and gradually more and more became aware of him. Finally two men stepped away from the others and walked over to meet him.

As the men approached, Clint noticed some of the carnival women, three of whom were very attractive, one full-figured and two very slender. The full-figured woman was blond and pretty and looked to be in her late thirties. The other two were dark-haired, obviously in their twenties, and might have been sisters. They all wore similar blouses and skirts. The blouses were off the shoulder and showed off some of their skin, with the blond woman having more to show off than the others. The dark-haired women had long necks and rather bony shoulders, while the blonde's neck swept down into an impressive display of cleavage. All three women were watching him as he reined in his team and prepared to speak to the men.

"Good afternoon," one of the men said, loudly but pleasantly.

Having never dealt with carnival people before, Clint didn't know what to expect, but he was glad that the man's tone sounded pleasant.

"Afternoon," Clint said. "I was just heading toward Benton's Fork when I saw your camp."

"You're welcome to step down and have a cup of coffee," the spokesman said. "We should have a pot going by now."

"That's real neighborly of you."

The man doing the talking looked about forty-five, with thick, steel-gray hair and a bushy mustache and sideburns to match. He was tall and well-built but with a paunch. The other man seemed to be a younger version, in his mid-thirties, hair also thick but dark, built along the same lines without the belly and the sideburns. He was studying Clint intently while his brother—Clint assumed they were brothers—did the talking.

Clint stepped down from his wagon, and all three men closed on each other, each taking a good look.

"My name's Clint Adams." He wondered if the carnival people would recognize it.

"My name is Fletcher Flora," the older man said, shaking Clint's hand, "and this is my brother, Frank."

Frank Flora just nodded.

"Come on," Fletcher said. "We're just setting up, but there should be coffee ready by now."

"I don't want to put you out," Clint said. "If you're not ready—"

"Nonsense," Fletcher said. "Carnival Flora is always ready to entertain."

They walked back toward a crowd of people who parted to let them through.

"We have a guest, everyone," Fletcher said, "but that's no excuse to stop working!"

They obeyed instantly. The two dark-haired women looked Clint up and down a moment before they moved along with the rest of the crowd. Clint noticed that the blond woman had already moved on.

He followed the Flora brothers to a camp fire, upon which not one but several pots of coffee rested.

"We drink a lot of it here," Fletcher explained. "How do you like it?"

"Strong and black," Clint said.

"Ah," Fletcher said, picking up one of the pots, "then you'll drink from my pot. That's the way I like my coffee as well."

Clint was soon to discover that this was not the only thing he and Fletcher Flora had in common.

# TWO

Clint sat at the camp fire with Fletcher Flora and his silent brother. Clint still couldn't figure out if Frank was just the quiet type or if the man was actually a mute.

"We think we have quite a show," Fletcher was saying.

"How does this differ from a circus?"

"It's smaller, naturally," the man said, "and our shows don't necessarily go on in a big tent, or in three rings. We do have a high wire act and a trapeze act, but other than that there's very little similarity. With us there's just a lot of different things going on at one time."

"Like with life," Clint observed.

Fletcher Flora laughed and said, "Exactly. Our new friend has a point, eh, Frank?"

The brother nodded.

"Frank, you'd better see that everything that should be getting done is getting done."

Frank nodded again and left.

"He's mute?" Clint asked.

"Yes," Fletcher said. "Which is why even though we're brothers I give the orders. How did you figure out he was mute and didn't just simply not want to speak?"

"He's too quiet," Clint said. "He would have grunted or replied in one way or another eventually, but he never made a sound."

"He grunts occasionally, but you're quite right. Usually he's extremely silent."

"How did it happen?"

Fletcher Flora spread his large, calloused hands and said, "No one knows. One day when he was eight, he just stopped talking, and never did again."

"Did your parents have him looked at by a doctor?" Clint asked.

"We didn't have parents," Fletcher said. "We were carnies, even then."

"Carnies?"

"It's what we call ourselves, we who live with the carnival."

"So did he ever see a doctor?"

"Several," Fletcher said. "I was eighteen at the time, and I insisted that he be seen by doctors. None of them could explain what had happened."

"That's an amazing story."

"Yes, it is," Fletcher agreed. "Quite amazing."

Clint sipped some coffee thoughtfully.

"So," Fletcher said, "how long are you planning to stay in Benton's Fork?"

"I don't really know."

"Are you going there to work?"

"If work is available," Clint said. "I'm a gunsmith."

"Ah," Fletcher said, "you repair guns?"

"That's right."

"Then perhaps I might have some work for you right here," the man said. "We have an act that involves guns. In fact, it might interest you."

"What kind of an act?"

"Sharpshooting. You would be surprised at some of the remarkable shots our people can make."

"I'm sure I would be."

"If you're here long enough, come and see the show," Fletcher said.

"Well, if it's as good as your coffee, it'll be worth coming to see."

"I'll make sure that you are not charged admission," Fletcher said. Then he added, "And if you wish to bring a friend . . ."

"I'm afraid I don't know anyone in Benton's Fork," Clint said.

Fletcher laughed.

"I don't think a man such as yourself would be alone very long," he said.

"I'll take that as a compliment," Clint said. He put his empty cup down and stood up. "When will you start your show?"

"Tomorrow morning we'll come into town and show some of our wares for free, and then we'll start performing in the afternoon."

"For free?"

"Just as an advertisement, you understand," Fletcher said. "Ah, baiting the hook."

"Oh, I see. Well, thank you for the coffee, Fletcher, and the hospitality."

"It was our pleasure," the man said.

As he stood, both he and Clint turned and saw the two dark-haired women watching from behind a wagon. When they realized that they had been seen, the women ducked out of sight.

"See what I mean about not being alone for long?" Fletcher asked. "Already you have aroused the interest of the twins."

"Twins?"

"Yes, Maria and Elena are twins."

"But they don't look exactly alike . . . do they?" Clint asked, wondering if he had missed that.

"They were born several minutes apart, which seems to have made some slight difference in their appearances. However, their talents and . . . appetites are as identical as can be."

"And what are their talents?"

"Oh, they do a high wire act," Fletcher said. "It's amazing to watch . . . and beautiful."

"I'm sure it is."

As they walked back to where Clint's rig was waiting, Fletcher asked, "Wouldn't you like to know about their appetites?"

"A man like me," Clint said, "would already know about that, wouldn't he?"

Fletcher laughed heartily for a moment.

"Yes," he agreed, still chuckling, "yes, I believe you would."

"Are they your star attractions?" Clint asked.

"No," Fletcher said, "believe it or not, they're not."

"Who is, then? The sharpshooters?"

"No," Fletcher said, shaking his head. "We picked up an act about a month ago which has been incredibly successful for us. His name is the Great Matthew."

"And what's so great about him?" Clint asked.

"Magic."

"Pardon me?"

"He is a magician. He does the most incredible magic you've ever seen."

"Oh, I see," Clint said. "He does illusions, tricks, stuff like that?"

"When you see him," Fletcher said, "you can tell me if you think the things he does are tricks or illusions. You will see for yourself."

When they were outside the circle of wagons, the two men shook hands and said good-bye again, but Clint still had something else on his mind.

"When I rode up, Fletcher," he said, "there was a blond woman here . . ."

"Ah," Fletcher said, with a smile, "don't say another word."

"You have only one blond woman with the carnival?" Clint asked.

"No," Fletcher said, "but only one who would catch your eye. Her name is Marthayn."

"Are you sure?" Clint asked. "She was a full-figured woman, very pretty, in her late thirties I'd say . . ."

"Marthayn," Fletcher said again, this time with a nod of his head.

"Marthayn," Clint repeated. "That's a pretty name . . . and unusual."

"She is an unusual woman."

"What does she do?" Clint asked. "I mean, for the carnival."

"My friend," Fletcher said, "you come back and she will tell you your future."

"My future?"

"If it is in the stars, and the moons, and the heavens," Fletcher said, "Marthayn will see it."

"Marthayn," Clint said again, as if tasting the name, then he headed for his rig.

As Clint climbed aboard his rig, Frank Flora once again appeared at the side of his brother. They both watched as Clint turned his team, and then Fletcher waved. Frank simply stared, and his eyes were black and cold . . . very, very cold.

Frank Flora did not strike Clint as the kind of man he could be friends with.

As Clint Adams rode away, Fletcher Flora said to his brother, "That is an interesting man, Frank. He just might be the man we are looking for."

Frank looked at him.

"Why?" Fletcher asked, voicing the other man's thoughts. He put his arm around his brother's shoulders and said, "Come with me and I will tell you why."

# THREE

Clint was still thinking about the blond woman, Marthayn, as he drove his rig down the main street of Benton's Fork. Later, after he had seen to the rig, the team, and Duke, his gelding, and he was in the hotel, he was still thinking about what Fletcher had said about her, that she would tell him his future. Clint had never before met a woman who could do that—or who claimed she could do that.

Of course, he did not believe in such things, and even if he did he wasn't sure he wanted someone to tell him his future. He had always felt he knew what his future was . . . a bullet in the back. He would never want that confirmed, though.

But since he didn't believe in such things, he was curious as to what she might have to say—

and he was curious about her. He was also curious about this magician, the Great Matthew. So, he was curious enough about everything to stay around a couple of days and take a look.

Staying around not only meant getting a room, it meant finding a place to have his meals, to get good coffee. It meant walking around town and getting to know where things were, and it meant stopping in to see the local sheriff, just to let him know he was there. It was a courtesy call he tried to make wherever he went.

As he entered the sheriff's office he saw that it looked much like all the others he had been in during his life, both as a visitor and as a lawman himself. A desk, a potbellied stove, a gun rack, and behind the desk a gray-haired man in his fifties who stood to greet him.

"Can I help you?"

"Sheriff . . ."

"Goodman," the man said. "Just get into town?"

"That's right, Sheriff Goodman," he said. "My name's Clint Adams."

The sheriff's reaction was immediate.

"Adams?"

"That's right."

"I've heard of you, of course," the man said. "What brings you to town?"

"The carnival," Clint said. The words were out of his mouth before he knew it.

"Carnival?" the sheriff said with a frown. "What carnival?"

"The one that's camped just outside of your town, to the north," Clint said. "I ran into them on the road, and they told me they'd be doing some performances hereabouts."

"Is that a fact?"

"There's no problem with that, is there, Sheriff?" Clint asked. He hoped he hadn't caused any trouble by mentioning it.

"No, no, no problem," Goodman said. "As long as they come into town first for a little talk."

"Oh, they'll be in," Clint said. "They told me that too."

"Well, that's good," Goodman said. "So you wouldn't have stopped in Benton's Fork if it wasn't for them?"

"I probably would have stopped, but not stayed over," Clint said.

"Like the carnival that much, do you?"

"I'm just curious, Sheriff," Clint said. "Which is probably the same thing that will bring a lot of people out to see it."

"I'm sure. Any idea how long you'll be staying, then?"

"Probably just a day or two."

"Well, Mr. Adams, I appreciate you stopping by and letting me know you're in town."

"My pleasure, Sheriff. Can you recommend a place for a good steak?"

"Sure," Goodman said, and gave Clint a couple of places, complete with directions.

As Clint headed for the door, Goodman said, "Ah, Mr. Adams . . ."

"Yes?"

"About your, uh, reputation . . ."

"I'm not looking for trouble, Sheriff," Clint said, "and I generally go out of my way to avoid it. Does that help?"

The sheriff looked relieved and said, "It helps quite a bit. Thanks."

"Sure," Clint said, and went out.

# FOUR

Fletcher Flora pushed back the flap of the tent and entered. The blond woman, Marthayn, looked up at him and frowned.

"What do you want?" she asked.

"Just hear me out for a moment," Fletcher said. "May I sit?"

"Do I have a choice?"

"As much of a choice as any of us have these days," Fletcher said.

"Which means none."

Fletcher took a seat across from her at the small table her crystal ball sat on. Of course she didn't really use the thing, but it was an effective prop.

"The man who was here today," Fletcher said, "I think he might be the answer to our problem."

16

"I noticed him."

"I knew that you did."

"Who is he?"

"His name is Clint Adams. Do you know the name?"

"Of course I do," she said. "I'm not stupid, Fletch."

"I know that, Marthayn," Fletcher Flora said. "I know that better than anyone."

"So you do."

They sat in silence for a while and then she asked, "How?"

"I don't know exactly how," Fletcher said. "But judging from his reputation, he's an extraordinary man."

"If you can believe his reputation."

"Even if only half of it's true, it's amazing," Fletcher said.

"How would you get him to help?"

"I don't know," he said. "Maybe Maria and Elena . . . they can be pretty persuasive when they want to be."

"I know that better than anyone," she said, with heavy irony.

"So you do."

Fletcher Flora, after all these months, was still only sorry that she had caught him. He was not sorry that he had taken both of the sisters to his bed. The experience had been worth it. Afterward, however, he did not have Marthayn anymore, and the sisters never came to his bed again.

Maybe he should have been sorry, but he wasn't. . . .

"So when will you ask him?"

"I don't know," he said. "I might need your help."

"You mean if Elena and Maria aren't as persuasive as they can be?"

"He expressed an interest in you."

"He did?" she said, showing some interest herself.

"He did."

"What did he ask?"

"Just who you were, and what you did."

"And?"

"And I told him that you would tell him something about his future."

"Like what?"

"Well," he said, "that's what I came here to talk to you about . . ."


After Fletcher spoke for five minutes he sat back and looked at Marthayn.

"What do you think?"

"I don't know," she said. "It all depends on how superstitious he is, I guess . . . and how smart."

"I'm betting that a man like him, who's lasted this long with the kind of reputation he has, believes in something a little more than luck."

"Yes," Marthayn said, "like maybe himself."

"And maybe a sixth sense," he said. "And anyone who believes in a sixth sense has an open mind."

"Okay, then," she said, "we have to hope he has an open mind."

"Right."

"Now what about Matthew?"

"What about him?"

"What's he going to think about Clint Adams?"

"We'll keep Adams away from him."

"But you said he was coming back to see the Great Matthew," Marthayn said. "How do you expect to keep Adams away from him?"

"For all Matthew will know, Adams is just another customer," Fletcher said, "another rube."

"Uh-huh," Marthayn said. "Aren't we forgetting one little thing?"

"Like what?"

"Like Matthew seems to have a little sixth sense of his own?"

Fletcher leaned forward again.

"This is too good an opportunity to pass up, Marthayn," Fletcher said. "We have to try it."

Marthayn hesitated a moment and then said, "Yes, you're right. We'll have to try it, and hope he doesn't get wind of it."

They both thought about it for a while, each knowing that the Great Matthew had already shown an aptitude for knowing things he shouldn't know, as well as doing things he shouldn't be able to do.

For that matter, doing things that no one should be able to do.

# FIVE

It was early the next morning when the Carnival Flora came into town.

Clint had spent the evening playing poker, and then the night with one of the saloon girls who took a fancy to him. He had explained that he didn't pay for sex, and she had explained that every so often it was nice to be with a man who wasn't paying her. They always thought it was her job to make them happy.

"Once in a while," she had told him, "I like to have a man make me happy."

"I think we'll be able to work together on this," he had said.

Clint sat up in bed the next morning and looked down at her. Her name was Jan, and she was a redhead who wore her hair short—

too short, he'd thought at first, but as the evening wore on the hairstyle had grown on him—as had the woman. She was a little older than the other girls in the place, and he generally liked women who were experienced.

She was lying on her belly, and the sheet was bunched up at her waist. Gently, he slid the sheet away from her so he could admire her firm butt and thighs and muscular calves. She had good legs, like most waitresses and saloon girls who spent most of their time on their feet.

He heard some noise from outside the window and realized that was what had woken him up. From the amount of light that was streaming into the room, he knew he had slept later than usual. He knew that was because he and Jan had slept very little during the night and had only drifted off to sleep early that morning.

Clint got up and padded naked to the window. He saw what looked like a parade going down the center of the main street. After a moment he realized it was a parade made up of the carnival performers.

He saw Fletcher Flora at the head of the column, and behind him several wagons with performers who were juggling, breathing fire, or simply waving. He saw the two sisters, Elena and Maria, sitting on swings that had been rigged to their wagon. They were attracting a lot of male attention, which was no doubt their job. He had to admit that even from his window they looked good.

"What's going on?" Jan asked sleepily from the bed.

"A parade."

"A what?"

"A parade," Clint said. He turned and looked at her and added, "There's a carnival in town."

"Is it worth me getting up to have a look?" she asked.

He looked down and saw that the only male performers in evidence were the skinny fellow doing the juggling and the fire-eater. There was no sign of the Great Matthew, or of any men who would be worth her while to walk to the window to see.

"No," he said, "stay in bed and sleep."

He turned to look at her then and saw that she had already fallen back to sleep.

He got dressed quietly and slipped from the room.

Down on the street he stopped to watch the parade going by. There were men dressed as clowns on each side of the street giving handwritten flyers to anybody who would take one. The flyers gave the name of the carnival, its location, and promised never-before-seen forms of entertainment.

Clint saw Sheriff Goodman across the street watching the proceedings, and he wondered if Fletcher Flora was intending to stop in and talk with the lawman. On the off chance that he wasn't, Clint decided to find the man and advise him to do so. He started walking up the street faster than the slow-moving parade, trying to catch up with the man.

Fletcher Flora, riding at the head of the parade, was disappointed not to see Clint Adams in the crowd somewhere along the way. He hoped that the man hadn't decided to keep moving on. Fletcher thought he had sufficiently aroused his interest to keep him there for at least one performance. He continued to swivel his head around, searching the crowd, when suddenly he heard his name being called out—and only one person in town knew his name!

"Fletcher!"

He turned his head and saw Clint Adams coming toward him.

"Clint. It's good to see you." Clint had no idea just how much Fletcher meant what he said.

"And you," Clint said, walking alongside Fletcher's horse, a big bay mare. "This is quite a little parade you have going here."

"Glad you like it."

"Not only me—the whole town seems to have turned out," Clint said. "Quite a feat for early morning."

"I like to do this kind of thing early," Fletcher explained. "If the town will wake up for this, they'll come out to see us."

"Sounds reasonable. But I hope you don't mind a little advice?"

"Of course not."

"You tell me if it's none of my business," Clint said, "but I think you'd be well advised to stop in and see the local law."

"It's very good advice," Fletcher said, "but it's something we do in every town we stop in, Clint. Thanks, anyway, for your concern."

"Of course," Clint said. "I should have known, you've been through this many times before."

"I'll be stopping by once we pass completely through the town," Fletcher said. "The others will return to where we've set up our tents. Have you had breakfast?"

"No, I haven't," Clint said. "But I hope you'll let me return your hospitality of yesterday by allowing me to buy you breakfast."

"If you'll still come out and see our performance, then yes."

"Oh, I'll be there," Clint said. "You can count on it."

"Good."

They agreed to meet at Clint's hotel when Fletcher was finished talking with the sheriff.

"I'll see you then." Clint moved off the street as the parade caught up and started to pass him again.

# SIX

Clint was sitting out in front of his hotel when Fletcher Flora crossed the street toward him. The parade had long since passed by, and the town was buzzing about the carnival. Almost everyone who passed Clint on the street was talking about it.

"I'm ready for that breakfast now," Fletcher said, rubbing his stomach. "I'm famished."

"Good," Clint said, standing up. "There's a small café down the street that was recommended to me yesterday—by the sheriff, as a matter of fact."

"Speaking of the sheriff," Fletcher said, "he was very . . . wary of me and my carnival—but then most people in authority are."

"Why is that?" Clint asked.

"Oh, I think they feel that a carnival atmosphere will interfere with the smooth operation of their town—you know, the everyday living."

"It's just a place for people to go and have a good time, have some fun," Clint said. "It's good for people to get out of their everyday routines once in a while."

"That's exactly what I told him," Fletcher said. "Maybe I should hire you to do public relations for the carnival, Clint."

"If I was looking for a job, I might take you up on that," Clint said.

Over breakfast Fletcher told Clint to call him "Fletch"; he said all his friends did. Clint was not quite ready to call Fletcher Flora a new friend, but he was willing to call him Fletch.

As they ate Fletcher told Clint about some more of the acts the carnival had and some of the places they had played. Apparently the Carnival Flora had concentrated on the midwest for quite a while before moving west, which probably explained why Clint—who traveled extensively throughout the west and southwest—had never heard of them.

"What time will your first performance be today?" Clint asked.

"Ah, you didn't get one of the flyers we made," Fletcher said, "and they're all gone. No problem. You already have a personal invitation. Our first performance will be at three o'clock this afternoon. Will you be coming?"

"I wouldn't miss it."

"And have you made a friend in town yet?"

"Ah . . . I've met someone, but I don't think she'll be coming with me."

"Well then, you'll have a good time out there all by yourself. I guarantee it."

After breakfast they parted company right outside the café.

"I have to get back to camp and make sure everything is ready for the performance."

"Isn't your brother there?"

"Yes, but I like to keep a personal eye on things—you know," Fletcher explained. "Besides, sometimes it takes a loud voice to keep the people moving."

"I see."

"Don't get me wrong," Fletcher said, "Frank does his part very well."

"I'm sure he does," Clint said.

"Yes, well, I have to get back. See you later?"

"I'll be there."

The two men shook hands, and then Clint watched as Fletcher walked to his horse, mounted up, and rode out of town.

Walking back to his hotel Clint wondered what he had done to deserve such preferential treatment.

Were carnies all that friendly?

He figured if he stuck around long enough, he'd find out—but did he want to?

When Fletcher Flora returned to camp, he found that things were progressing smoothly

for the afternoon's performance. He turned his
horse over to the nearest man and walked over
to his brother, who apparently heard him coming and turned.

"I'm back," Fletcher said, unnecessarily.

Frank just looked at him, but Fletcher was
able to read the look.

"Yes," he said, "Clint Adams will be coming
to the performance. I have to tell Marthayn to
be ready for him."

Frank frowned.

"I don't know if this is going to work, Frank,"
Fletcher said. "I suppose we'll have to find out.
Uh, where is he?"

Frank turned and nodded toward the Great
Matthew's private wagon.

"He hasn't come out since we got here, has
he?"

Frank shook his head.

"Not even to eat?"

Another shake.

Fletcher Flora shivered and went to find
Marthayn.

# SEVEN

Clint was impressed by the turnout for the first performance of the Carnival Flora. He was also impressed by the carnival's choice of a place to set up. He hadn't noticed before but they had set up in a pretty open field, with no trees or boulders to get in their way. Also, off to one side was a hill where people could sit and watch what was going on without getting in each other's way. It was smart. It prevented fights from breaking out because someone couldn't see over someone else's head.

The entire carnival was set up in a circle, and people had to buy tickets to get inside. The circle was tied off, and every so often there was a man—usually a big man—standing guard to keep people—mostly kids—from sneaking in without paying.

Clint, of course, was admitted without paying, which made some of the other people look at him strangely. Clint found it strange that he hadn't had to identify himself to the man selling the tickets. The man had simply smiled and said, "Enjoy the show, Mr. Adams."

Once inside the circle Clint saw that there were many different attractions set up, usually out of or in front of a wagon. In a few places tents had been set up, and something was either going on outside or inside.

He saw jugglers, sword swallowers, fireeaters; there was even a man juggling flaming swords.

Behind the circle was a larger tent which reminded him of the circus. Inside was probably where the trapeze acts were performed, but the tent was nowhere near as large as some of the tents he'd seen at the circus.

There were also venders selling different kinds of food and sweets, as well as beverages—punch, sarsaparilla, and plenty of beer. He wondered how the saloon owners in town would feel about that.

He was debating having a beer himself when he felt someone touch him on the arm. He turned and looked into a very pretty face framed by blond hair that glowed in the sunlight.

"You're Clint Adams," she said.

"That's right."

"I'm Marthayn," she said. "I understand I'm supposed to tell you about your future."

"Really?"

She frowned.

"That's what Fletch told me," she said. "Am I . . . mistaken?"

"No, no," he said hurriedly. "He said the same thing to me."

"Oh, good," she said, "I thought maybe I was wrong. Are you ready?"

"Well, I don't know," Clint said. "Fletch told me about this, but I wasn't really sure I was going to do it."

"And why not?"

"Well . . ."

"You're not afraid, are you?"

He shook his head and said, "Afraid isn't the word I'd use."

"What then?"

He stared at her for a moment.

"What do you know about me?"

"Do you mean, do I know that you're called the Gunsmith?"

"Yes."

"Well, of course I do."

"Then you know the kind of life I've led."

"I know the kind of life you're supposed to have led," she said. "I don't always believe what I hear. That's neither here nor there, though. What's your point?"

"Well, I've always thought that I knew how I would die," he said. "Living the way I have, I mean, and having seen how some of my friends have died . . ."

She held up her hand for him to stop and said, "Let me put your mind at rest. One of the things I do not tell people is how or when they are going to die."

"Even if you know?"

"Even if I know," she said.

"What else don't you tell them?"

"Nothing," she said. "Everything else is fair game, don't you think?" She smiled.

"I guess so."

"Are you ready then?"

He looked at her face, her eyes, her hair. She was about five four, probably in her late thirties, and she was wearing a rather large, billowy dress that might have been designed to hide her figure. But it could not hide the fullness of her breasts. He could only guess about the rest of her, but what he saw he liked very much.

"Why not?" he said.

"Good. Come with me, then."

"Where?"

"I don't do this out in the open, I do it in my tent," she said. "We'll have to go there. You don't have a problem being alone with me in my tent, do you?"

He laughed.

"No," he said, "no problem at all."

"Good," she said, "then come this way. . . ."

# EIGHT

Clint entered Marthayn's tent, which was not one of the larger ones in the carnival.

When he commented on that, she said, "I don't need as much room as sword swallowers and fire-eaters to do what I do. Also, I don't need that much room to sleep."

There was a small table in the center of the tent with a chair on either side. On the table was a big glass ball.

"What's that?" he asked.

"What?"

He pointed at the ball.

"Oh, that," she said. "That's a crystal ball."

"What's it for?"

"Sit down," Marthayn said. She sat and he took the other chair and stared at her.

"I'm supposed to be able to look into this

crystal ball and see the future," she explained.

"Supposed to?"

"Well, it doesn't always work."

"What does?"

"Nothing always works," she said.

"Are you supposed to admit that?"

She smiled and said, "Probably not. Tell me something, will you?"

"If I can."

"Why aren't you more skeptical?" she asked. "You're not scoffing at this."

"Why should I?"

"Most people do," she said.

"How do you make a living, then?"

"Oh, don't get me wrong," she answered. "A lot of people believe that I can do what I do. Some don't believe it, but they pay to have their futures told anyway, just as a joke."

"Does that bother you?"

"There's two ways to answer that."

"What are they?"

"One, I don't care if they believe or not, as long as they pay."

"And the other?"

"Maybe it would bother me if I really thought I could do what I do."

"Which answer do you use?"

"The first one," she said. "The second one would put me out of business."

"I guess it would. Well, how do you propose to tell my future?"

"Give me your hand," she said. "The right one, palm up."

He extended the hand to her, and she took it in hers and stared down at it. She turned it over and looked at the back first.

"The back of your hand tells me your characteristics, your traits, what kind of a man you are."

"Uh-huh."

"I can also see here that you have the same powers that I do."

"I do?"

"Oh, yes. Many people do, in fact, it's just that they don't know how to develop them."

"Uh-huh," he said, for want of something else to say.

"The back of the left hand tells me what you could have done with your life and did not. The back of the right hand tells me what you've done with your life up to now, and what you will do with your life in the future."

"I see."

"I can see that you're a very independent man, very set in your ways."

Clint did not respond.

"Once you make up your mind to do something, you generally do it."

"Mmm-hmm."

"No relationships at the moment, is that right?"

"No permanent relationships, no."

"I do see a woman here," she said, "a red-haired woman who wears a gun. Do you know someone like that?"

He did, in fact. Anne Archer was a red-haired

woman who worked as a bounty hunter.

"I do."

"You could be close with this woman, but you choose not to be. Why is that?"

"There's just a lot of space between us."

"Literally speaking?"

"Yes."

"All right," she said, "we won't get into that, then. All I'll say is that I don't see marriage in your immediate future."

"Neither do I."

"Good," she said, "then we're in agreement. I see you have a nice, outgoing personality . . . when you want to. At other times you can be a very private person, even a moody person."

Again he remained silent.

"I see a weakness in your lower back. . . ."

"Not to my knowledge."

She smiled.

"If you don't now, you will later on."

"Oh."

She turned his hand over and looked at the front. She touched her finger to the longest line on his hand.

"Every fourth of an inch is five years of your life," she said.

"Interesting."

"This is when you were about twenty-five years old," she said. "This is when you first became serious about guns—using them and fixing them."

"You're right," he said, wondering if she could have read that somewhere.

"And I see no major break in your line of fate," she went on. "I see guns in your future, as well."

He nodded, studying her face as she studied his hand. There was a line between her eyes when she concentrated.

"I see a . . . a terrible shock right here, some years back. I would say you were in your late thirties when this occurred. You lost a friend . . . violently, and you did not react well."

Clint was stunned. She was talking about the death of Wild Bill Hickok, his good friend. Hickok had been shot in the back and killed, and she was right, Clint had not taken the news well.

"I see I'm correct."

"Y-yes."

"All right," she said, "to the future, then. As I said, I don't see marriage, I see guns . . . and I see . . . a man."

"A man?" he asked. "What man?"

She stared down at his hand for a few moments, then released it and sat back.

"I'm finished."

"What? Finished? What about the man?"

"I can't see him clearly."

"You can't see clearly," he said. "You look like you've seen a ghost."

"No, not a ghost. . . ."

"Describe him for me."

"Mr. Adams—"

"Clint."

"Clint—"

"Go ahead, Marthayn," he said, "describe him."

She frowned and then took his hand again.

"He's a big man, heavy but not tall, not young, not old, somewhere in the middle . . . bearded, a heavy beard . . . dark eyes, black . . . and a black soul . . . very black . . . an evil man with whom you will clash . . . violently. . . ."

She released his hand and sat back again.

"That's all."

"Doesn't sound like anyone I know."

"It isn't," she said. "He's in your future."

"How far in the future?"

She hesitated, then said, "Not far."

"How far is not far?"

"Almost immediate," she said.

"I see," he said. "Within the next couple of weeks?"

"Days," she said.

"Uh-huh."

"Maybe hours."

"Maybe right outside your tent?" he asked.

She glared at him and said, "I don't know. I'm only telling you what I saw."

"A big man with whom I'll clash violently," he repeated.

"Yes."

"All right," he said, "give me your hand now."

"What?"

"Your hand," he said. "You said I had the power. I want to see if I do."

"This is silly—"

"Are you afraid?" he asked. "Is that it?"

"No," she said, "of course not."

"Then give me your hand."

She continued to hesitate.

"Come on. . . ."

She sat forward and reluctantly extended her hand to him. He took it in his, palm up, and examined it.

"Let's see . . ."

# NINE

"What do you see?" she asked.

"I see a man in *your* future."

"Oh?"

"A tall man, not young, not old, not unattractive . . ."

"I see," she said, starting to catch on. "And what do you see me doing with this man?"

"Oh, not much, at first," he said. "I see . . . a meal."

"Breakfast?" she asked, teasing.

"Oh, no," he said, "dinner . . . definitely dinner first."

"When is this supposed to happen?"

He looked at her face and asked, "Tonight?"

"I don't know. . . ."

"Well, I know," he said, looking back at her

hand. He tapped the center of her palm with his forefinger and said, "It says right here that you'll have dinner tonight . . . with me."

He looked at her, and she hesitated before saying, "Well, I guess if it says it there, I don't have much choice, do I?"

"No," he said, "I guess you don't."

"I'll walk you out," she said. "I'm supposed to be working."

"I'll come by when you're finished," he said as they walked to the entrance of the tent. "When will that be?"

"Not for a few hours, I'm afraid."

"Well," he said, "I'll be around. There's a lot here for me to see."

"Oh, yes," she said, "I think I can safely say you'll see something that will interest you."

"Is that a prediction," he asked, "or a promise?"

She smiled and said, "Call it a hunch."

He put his hand out and she took it.

"Until later," he said. "I'll go out now and maybe I'll find that man you told me about."

He started to release her hand, but she held on to his tightly.

"You have to be careful, Clint," she said. "Very careful."

"I always am, Marthayn," he said, sliding his hand free. "Don't worry."

As Clint exited the tent he squinted against the bright sunlight and saw a man approaching him. For a moment he thought it was Fletcher

Flora, but as the man came closer he saw that it was his brother.

"Hello, Frank," Clint said. He wasn't sure whether or not the man had intended to stop, but he did when Clint spoke to him. Unfortunately, all he did was stare.

"I've only been here a short while," Clint said, "but so far I'm finding it very interesting."

For a moment he didn't think the man was going to react at all, but finally Frank nodded his head. His expression never changed, though. Clint couldn't imagine what Frank Flora must look like when he smiled—if he ever smiled.

"Well," Clint said, tired of carrying on a conversation with himself, "I guess I'll keep walking around. There's a lot to see, isn't there?"

Frank nodded, but didn't move, so it was Clint who started walking. He did not turn to see if the man was watching him.

He felt very foolish being intimidated by a man who couldn't talk, but he couldn't deny that he was.

It was odd, very odd.

# TEN

Clint spent some time looking at some of the smaller attractions, and then an announcement was made by Fletcher Flora that the trapeze act was about to start.

Maria and Elena were introduced as two Gypsy princesses from Europe who came to this country to avoid persecution when their parents were killed during a takeover—a "coup" Fletcher called it—in their country.

"And now," Fletcher said dramatically, "the beautiful Federoyev sisters."

Clint recognized the name as Russian, but to him Maria and Elena looked suspiciously Mexican in origin.

They were beautiful, though, there was no denying that, and talented. They performed

individually and together. Clint admired the
muscles in their shoulders, arms, and legs as
they performed in two swings suspended about
fifty feet off the ground.

At one point Maria had her legs wrapped
around Elena's waist—or the other way
around—and a man behind Clint said, "I
wish I could get her to wrap her legs around
my waist like that."

"Yeah," another man said, "my wife can't do
that at all."

Obviously, the sisters were capturing the
attention—and the imagination—of every man
in the audience, including Clint. He found himself watching the sisters perform, watching the
way the muscles moved in their arms and
thighs, and wondering what it would be like
to be in bed with them—either one at a time
or together.

He knew every other man in the audience
was imagining the same scenario.

The women were also watching the sisters
intently. Maybe some of them wished they
were like them, or maybe they were just
enjoying the performance. He even saw some
of the women looking at their husbands as
the men watched the two women twirling.
There were women there who were jealous,
entranced, and perhaps even envious of the
two sisters.

He looked off to one side and saw Fletcher
Flora watching the sisters perform, and he wondered if the man had had one of the sisters or

both. Or had he been involved with Marthayn? Or all three, at different times? Fletcher was certainly a man women would be interested in—plus the fact that he was in a position of authority.

When the performance was over, the people filed out of the tent, all talking about what they had seen. The comments that Clint heard were mixed.

"Beautiful women . . ." a man was saying.

"How do they stretch like that?" a woman asked.

"A lot of nerve . . ." a boy said.

A woman said the same thing in a different tone of voice. "Lot of nerve . . . brazen hussies . . ." She sniffed after she said it.

For the most part, though, the comments were highly positive.

"I think they enjoyed it."

Clint turned and found Fletcher Flora standing next to him.

"I'm sure they did."

"And you?"

"Oh, I enjoyed it very much," Clint said. "In fact, I was fascinated."

"Would you like to meet them?" Fletcher asked. "The sisters?"

Clint hesitated, and then said, "Not if you expect me to believe they're Russian."

Fletcher laughed.

"I wouldn't expect to be able to fool you that way, Clint," Fletcher said.

"Mexican?"

The other man nodded.

"And it's taken me forever to work on their accents," Fletcher said. "Care to hear?"

"Lead the way," Clint said.

# ELEVEN

Fletcher led Clint around behind the big tent. There was a wagon there which was not part of the circle. Obviously, if the sisters were not the star performers of the carnival they were pretty close.

"What about your star?" Clint asked as they approached the wagon.

Fletcher stopped short.

"What about him?"

"The magician, the Great Matthew," Clint said. "When does he go on?"

"Oh," Fletcher said, and Clint thought he felt the man relax for some reason. "He should be going on in about an hour. He knows he's the star, you know, and you can't rush him."

Clint nodded, but he felt that if Fletcher was

the boss, he should have been able to rush anyone he wanted to.

"Did you see Marthayn?" Fletcher asked.

"I did."

"And?"

"And what?"

Fletcher stopped again. They were almost to
the wagon, but he turned and stared at Clint.

"Did she foretell your future?"

"She told me a bit about myself, and my
past," Clint said, "and yes, something about
the future."

"Ah," Fletcher said, widening his eyes, "something exciting, or frightening?"

"I thought you were going to let me meet the
sisters," Clint said.

"Ah, you're so right," Fletcher said, putting
his hand on Clint's shoulder. "It's none of my
business. Come on, then. We'll see if they're
decent."

They walked up to the wagon, which had
THE FEDEROYEV SISTERS painted on the wood-
en side. He followed Fletcher to the door in the
back and waited as the man knocked.

"Come on, girls," Fletcher yelled, "it's the
boss out here."

Fletcher turned and smiled at Clint, and then
turned back as the door opened.

One of the sisters appeared in the doorway.
She was still dressed for her act and was wiping
perspiration from her forehead with a towel.
Her shoulders and cleavage were exposed, and
glistened with sweat. Clint felt something tight-

en inside him when her eyes met his and she smiled.

"Maria, meet my friend, Clint Adams," Fletcher said.

"Hello," she said, with hardly a trace of any accent, Mexican or Russian. "I remember you when you rode up yesterday."

Apparently, Fletcher had trained the accent right out of her.

"Where's your sister, honey?" Fletcher asked.

"Inside," Maria said, still holding Clint's eyes. "I'll get her."

She patted the side of her neck with the towel and backed out of sight, leaving the door open. Moments later the other sister appeared. Her skin and hair were as dark as Maria's and her flesh was also glistening, but Clint noticed that she had a slightly wider mouth and longer neck.

"Elena," Fletcher said, "Clint Adams. He enjoyed your act very much."

"Thank you, Mr. Adams," Elena said. There was a hint of accent in her voice, which Clint caught, but which someone else might not have.

"You and your sister are . . . amazing," Clint said.

Elena smiled and caused the same tightening in his stomach as her sister had.

"Yes," she said, holding his eyes, "we are."

"Clint, after the show we'll be having some dinner. Would you stay and have some with us?"

"Well," Clint said, "I did have—"

"The girls would like you to stay . . . wouldn't you, girls?"

Maria stuck her head out the door and said, "Yes, we would . . . very much."

Elena added, "Please stay."

"We won't take no for an answer," Fletcher said.

"Well . . . all right," Clint said. He'd explain it to Marthayn. In a way they'd still be having dinner together.

Then again, if she could see the future, she probably knew already.

# TWELVE

"I think they like you," Fletcher said as they walked away from the wagon.

"How could you tell?"

Fletcher laughed.

"They didn't use their accents."

"Do they really have Russian accents?"

The man laughed again.

"I've never been to Russia, have you?"

"No."

"I've never even met a Russian," Fletcher added, "have you?"

"Well, yeah, I have."

Fletcher slapped him on the back and said, "That's perfect. You can tell me if they have real Russian accents."

Clint laughed now.

"I'll do my best," he said, "even though it's been a while since I spoke to anyone."

"Good, good," Fletcher said. "Now it's time for a treat."

"You mean this wasn't a treat?"

"These ladies are a real treat," Fletcher said. "I know . . . and maybe you'll find out, huh?"

"Maybe," Clint said as they walked back around the big tent. "To tell you the truth, I was planning on having dinner with someone else tonight."

"Oh? Who?"

"Marthayn."

Fletcher looked surprised and stroked his chin with his thumb and forefinger.

"Really?"

"Yes."

"You don't waste much time, do you?"

Clint stopped short and looked at Fletcher.

"Wait a minute . . . are you and she, uh . . ."

"Oh, no, no, nothing like that," Fletcher said. "Well, maybe at one time, but not now. I, uh, sort of ruined that with Elena and Maria, you know?"

"I think I get the idea."

"I'm sorry if I ruined your dinner plans," Fletcher said, "but I think Marthayn will understand."

"I hope so."

"Right now," Fletcher said, putting his hand on Clint's arm, "that treat I was talking about."

"Which is what?"

Fletcher made a grand gesture with his arms, a wide, sweeping motion, and said, "The Great Matthew is about to go on."

# THIRTEEN

The stage for the Great Matthew was an extension of his wagon. The wooden side of the wagon came down on hinges, and the magician stepped out from behind a black curtain. He was wrapped in a black cape with a white shirt beneath it, black tie, pants, and shoes.

"The Great Matthew!" Fletcher announced.

Matthew appeared to be in his late thirties, even though his beard had a streak of gray in it. His dark eyebrows had an upward cast to them at the end, giving him a satanic appearance. Clint wondered if they were naturally like that, or if he had trimmed them that way.

Matthew made a motion with his arm and suddenly flames seemed to leap from his hand. The crowd gasped. Clint didn't know how the man had done it, but he knew it had to be a trick. Still, in the waning light of dusk, it was very effective.

Matthew went into his act then, and Clint found it odd that the man worked silently. He wondered if Matthew was as mute as Frank Flora was.

Clint had seen medicine drummers and sales-men of all kinds, and even performers on the stage in New York, San Francisco, St. Louis, and Denver, and very few of them performed in silence. Most of them needed to sell them-selves verbally, but the Great Matthew seemed perfectly capable of holding his audience in the palm of his hand without uttering a word.

Clint watched in fascination as Matthew per-formed. He made things burst into flames, he made things disappear, he made things float. It was the floating that really surprised Clint, even more than when Matthew made a pony disappear.

When the magician finished his act and the side of the wagon was folded back up, the crowd remained in a stunned silence for a few moments, and then they started to applaud. Some of them even shouted.

Fletcher Flora sidled up to Clint afterward. The man looked more serious than Clint had ever seen him before.

"What did you think?" he asked.

"He's amazing," Clint said. "How did he . . ."

"How did he what?"

"Well . . . the floating thing, how did he do that?" Clint asked.

"You found that more interesting than making the pony disappear?"

"Well, that was incredible, of course," Clint said. "How did he do that?"

"I don't know."

"Well then, how did he do the floating thing? I mean, I know it's a trick, but how—"

"I don't know."

"You don't know?"

Fletcher shrugged.

"Matthew is very good at what he does, Clint," Fletcher said.

"But even you don't know how he does his tricks?" Clint asked.

"Uh, no . . ."

"But you're the boss."

"Well," Fletcher said, "I don't quite know how Elena and Maria do what they do. I run the carnival, but the performers are in charge of their own acts."

"I see."

"Are you ready for some food?"

"Uh, well, I haven't spoken to Marthayn yet."

"I spoke to her."

"You did?"

"Yes," Fletcher said, "I explained that you'd be eating with all of us tonight. You and she can eat together another time."

"She's not upset about that?"

"She's fine," Fletcher said. "I'm the boss, remember?"

"Yeah, sure."

"Let's go this way," Fletcher said, pointing. "We'll be setting up for supper. We have a really good cook."

"Okay, just lead the way."

They began walking away from the crowd, which was starting to file out. The Great Matthew had been the final act of the day.

"You have sharp eyes, Clint," Fletcher said.

"I do?"

"You must, in order to do what it is you do."

"And what's that?"

"Well, you're good with a gun," Fletcher said. "You can hit what you aim at almost every time."

"Point."

"What?"

"I hit what I point at," Clint said. "You don't aim a gun, you point it."

"I see," Fletcher said. "Well, whatever, you do have sharp eyes."

"What are you getting at?"

Fletcher stopped and faced Clint.

"What did you see when you were watching Matthew?" he asked.

"What do you mean, what did I see?" Clint asked. "I saw what everybody else saw."

"No, I don't think so," Fletcher said. "I think with your eyes you might have seen more than anyone else."

"Like what?"

Fletcher seemed to be at a loss for words for just a moment. "I'm not sure," he finally said. "To tell you the truth, I wish I did

know how Matthew does his . . . his tricks, his
magic, his . . . his act! But I simply can't figure
them out."

"Why don't you ask him?"

Fletcher looked shocked at the suggestion,
and for a moment Clint thought the man might
be afraid of the magician.

"I did," Fletcher said, but Clint thought he
was lying. "He won't talk."

"And you can't see how he does them?"

"No."

"And you think I can?"

Fletcher waved his arms and said, "I think
you might be able to, yes."

"What are you saying, exactly, Fletch?"

"I'd like you to watch him again tomorrow,
and watch more closely," Fletcher said. "I want
you to tell me what you see."

Clint thought it over.

"Do you think you could do that?"

"I don't know," Clint said. "Do you mean,
could I do it, or will I do it?"

"I guess I mean, will you do it?"

Clint thought a moment longer, wondering
why he should get involved with this—and the
reason he came up with was the same reason
he had stayed to see the carnival . . . curiosity.
What was the harm?

"All right."

"You'll do it?"

"Sure, why not? I'll give it a try. I'm very
curious about how he does what he does."

"This is wonderful," Fletcher said. "Mat-

thew's been with us for a few months and
no one has been able to figure out how he
does what he does."

"There must be a way to figure these things
out," Clint said. "I mean, clearly he can't be
doing these things for real. . . ."

Fletcher didn't reply.

"Wait a minute," Clint said, "you can't tell me
that you people think that he really does . . .
magic?"

The man didn't answer.

"Fletch?"

For a moment Fletcher looked like he was
going to reply, then he stopped and turned
away.

"Let's go see if the food is ready."

# FOURTEEN

When Clint and Fletcher reached the place where supper was being prepared, there was a crowd of people already there, but a totally different crowd than had been gathered to watch Matthew perform. These, Clint saw, were the carnies.

He saw the sword swallower without a sword in his mouth, the fire-eater with no flames, Elena and Maria without their limbs locked together on a swing fifty feet above the ground. What he didn't see was the magician, Matthew.

He did see Marthayn, though, and she gave him a knowing look.

"Where's Matthew?" Clint asked Fletcher.

"He, uh, doesn't eat with the rest of us."

"He doesn't?"

"No."

"Where does he eat?"

Fletcher turned around and handed Clint a wooden bowl filled with steaming stew.

"Looks great," Clint said. "So where does he eat?"

"In his wagon, I guess."

"You guess?" Clint asked. "Are you telling me you've never seen him eat?"

"Uh, well, yes, that's right," Fletcher said.

"Wait a minute—"

"Let's sit down somewhere," Fletcher said, carrying his own stew.

They moved away from the line of people waiting to have their bowls filled and found someplace to sit. They had just sat down when Marthayn came walking over with two cups of coffee.

"How did you know?" Clint asked.

"Silly question," she said, handing him his coffee and walking away. He wondered if she was angry with him. Not that he felt anger coming from her, but maybe he wanted her to be angry—or at least disappointed.

"She's a lovely woman," Fletcher said.

"Yes, I agree," Clint said. "Fletch, tell me about Matthew."

"What do you want to know?"

"Is Matthew his real name?"

"I don't know."

"Wait a minute, he works for you and you don't know his real name?"

"No."

"Where's he from?"

Fletcher shrugged. "He just showed up one day and said he wanted to be in the carnival. He showed me some of his act, and I hired him."

"Is that the way it's usually done?"

"Look around you," Fletcher said.

Clint did. He saw a variety of people unlike any he had ever seen before. From across the way Marthayn was watching him and Fletcher, and from another side of the compound Elena and Maria were watching him. The others were concentrating on their food, and not giving him a second thought. At that moment Clint realized that Fletcher's brother was not around.

"Where's Frank?" he asked.

"He's probably making sure nobody tried to stay behind," Fletcher said. "Sometimes kids try to hide and stay behind. If they do, Frank scares them away. He can be pretty scary."

"Tell me some more about Matthew."

"What can I tell you? I don't *know* anything about Matthew," Fletcher said. "If you watch him work tomorrow, maybe you'll know more about him than I do."

"Maybe I will," Clint said. "Tell me something."

"What?"

"Are you sorry you ever took him on?"

Fletcher laughed, but there was no humor in it.

"I'm sorry I took half these people on, Clint," he said. "Almost every day."

They finished eating, and Clint got up to get himself another cup of coffee. He was reaching for the pot when a woman's hand got to it before he did.

"I will pour," Elena said.

Up close her face was devastating. Her eyes were very dark, as were her eyebrows. Her skin was dark too. She was possibly the darkest woman he had ever seen who wasn't actually a black woman.

"Thank you."

He held his cup out, and she poured until it was full to the brim.

"Just black, right?"

"That's right."

She put the pot back.

"I noticed how you drank it."

"You're very observant."

"Yes," she said. "I am. For instance, I was watching you as you watched us do our act today."

"You were able to do what you were doing and still watch me?"

"Oh, yes," she said.

"How?"

"I was very interested in you."

"Really?"

"And so was my sister," she added. "We were both watching you."

Clint laughed.

"I'm surprised you and your sister didn't fall off the swing."

"Trapeze," she said. "It's called a trapeze."

Clint wondered what a couple of Mexican sisters knew about a trapeze.

"I'm flattered, Elena," he said. "I'm very flattered."

She smiled at him, then turned and walked back to where her sister was sitting.

Clint took his coffee back to Fletcher and sat with the man.

"I'm going to finish this and then get going," he said.

"You'll be back tomorrow?"

"I'll be back."

Clint finished his coffee, put the cup down, and started to walk away.

"Hey, Clint?" Fletcher called.

"Yeah?"

"How did you like the carnival?"

"I liked it," Clint said, "I liked it a lot."

# FIFTEEN

Fletcher watched Clint walk away, the last rube to leave the carnival grounds. Now it was all carnies. He looked around for Frank and didn't see him, but he knew his brother would be along any minute.

He thought about what Clint had asked him, about being sorry he'd taken Matthew on as an act. Hell, he'd been sorry the very next week, when he realized that the Great Matthew was not just an act he had taken on, he was a curse— a curse he hoped Clint Adams was going to help him get rid of.

Fletcher caught Elena's eye and beckoned to her with a wave of his hand. She left her sister's side and walked over to him. He took her hand.

"You know what to do?"

"Yes," Elena said, "we know."

"Good."

"When do you want us to do it?"

"Tonight."

"Tonight?"

"That's right, tonight."

The girl gave him a frightened look and asked, "Do you think he knows?"

"Elena, honey," Fletcher said, squeezing her hand, "I don't know what he knows. Just do it, okay?"

"All right, Fletch," she said, "we'll do it."

"Good."

As soon as Elena went back to sit by her sister, Marthayn approached him.

"Are you sending them?"

"Yes."

"How did I know that?"

"You know everything, don't you?" he asked.

"Not everything."

"Damn right," he said. "If you knew everything, you would have told me to send Matthew packing when he first showed up."

She laughed softly and said, "You can't blame me for Matthew, Fletch."

"No," Fletcher said, "I can't blame anyone but myself."

He looked past her and saw Frank coming toward him.

"Do me a favor, Marthayn, and get Frank something to eat, huh?"

"Sure, Fletch."

As she walked away, Frank reached him.

"Is he in his wagon?" Fletcher asked.

Frank nodded, then raised his eyebrows at his brother.

"Yes," Fletcher said, "Clint Adams was very interested in Matthew. I asked him to come back and watch his act again, to see if he could pick up how he was doing his . . . his tricks."

Frank looked surprised, then asked his brother another question with just a glance.

"Does he believe me?"

Frank nodded.

"Yeah, he believed me," Fletcher said. "He thinks that's all I want from him."

Marthayn returned with a bowl of stew for Frank, who took it without looking at her. She gave each of the brothers a look, then turned and walked away. Frank sat down on the ground at his brother's feet to eat his supper.

The carny boss wondered what Matthew was doing in his wagon right at that moment. The only time the man came out was when he did his act. Fletcher had not spoken to the man more than once a week since his arrival. Matthew was as much a mystery now as he had been when he first arrived—even more so.

More of a mystery, and more of a curse than ever.

# SIXTEEN

When Clint got back to town, he spent the evening playing poker, even though his mind wasn't on the game. At one point he remembered a card trick that the Great Matthew had done, and he wished that he could perform a similar trick on the bad hand he was holding.

Luck was with him more than skill, though, and when he left the saloon, he had only lost a few dollars.

It was after eleven when he got back to his room. He unstrapped his gun belt and hung it on the bedpost, then removed his shirt and boots and sat on the bed.

He thought about the Great Matthew and the tricks he had seen the man perform that day. He couldn't believe that Fletcher and his people—seasoned carnies—would believe that

Matthew could actually perform feats of magic.
There had to be tricks to the man's illusions,
and Clint was taking it as sort of a challenge
to try and spot them. Tomorrow he'd watch
the man's hands a lot more closely than he
had today.

He wondered if Fletcher Flora had had this
in mind all along, from the moment they first
met, or had he thought of it later, when he
realized who Clint was?

And who was to say that this was all that the
man wanted from him? Except what else could
there be?

He was about to recline on the bed when
there was a knock on his door. He stood up,
took his gun from his holster, and carried it to
the door with him. A knock at the door late at
night—who knew what it could be? He had not
lasted this long by being careless.

"Who is it?"

"Elena."

"Elena?" he repeated to himself.

He unlocked the door and opened it. Not only
was Elena standing in the hall, but Maria as
well.

"What are you two doing here?" he asked.

"Can we come in . . . please?" Elena asked.

"It's late—"

"Please," Maria said.

"All right," he said, and backed away from
the door to allow them to enter.

Elena entered first, followed by Maria, who
closed the door behind her.

Clint walked over to the bedpost and replaced the gun in the holster. He turned to face the two sisters then.

"What are you doing here, ladies?"

They were both wearing dresses with shawls drawn across their shoulders. However, the demure quality of their clothes could not hide the pure wantonness that they exuded from every pore. In the confines of the small room, Clint could feel himself reacting to them. His body seemed to have a mind of its own.

"I told you earlier tonight," Elena said, very carefully, "we are interested in you."

"Very interested," Maria said.

Clint was sure that the preciseness of their speech came from long practice to hide their accents—their Mexican accents.

"Elena, Maria, I am very flattered . . . or am I? Did Fletcher send you?"

"No one sent us," Elena said. "We came on our own."

"Won't you be missed?"

"By whom?" she asked.

"By the others?"

"There are no others in our wagon," Elena said. "Only we know if we are there or not."

"Look, girls—"

"Enough talk," Maria said.

Before Clint had time to react, Maria's shawl was off and her dress was down around her ankles. While he was staring at Maria's sleek, svelte body, her sister also dropped her clothing, and they both stood there gloriously naked.

"Oh, what the hell," Clint said, and in record time he removed the remainder of his clothes. . . .

The way it all took place seemed to him later to have been like a slow dream. . . .

The women moved to him, and suddenly it was as if he was being worshipped. One girl on each side, they began to cover his body with kisses, explore it with tongues and teeth, and then they centered on his penis, which was full and pulsating. First one sister took it in her mouth and sucked on it, then the other took over. They alternated that way for a while until he thought his whole body would explode. At one point Elena was sucking on his penis while Maria was down between his legs licking and fondling his testicles. . . .

Soon they stood up and pushed him down on the bed. It was obvious to Clint that they were intent on being in charge, but he decided to turn the tables on them. He rolled away from them, causing both of them to look surprised.

"On your back," he commanded, and since neither sister was quite sure which one he was talking to, they looked at each other and then Elena lay down on her back.

Clint had been to bed with two women before, but never sisters. In the past, on one or two occasions, the women had gotten involved to the point of making love with each other, as well. He didn't expect that here, so he assumed he'd have to pay equal attention to both women.

"You too," he told Maria, and she promptly lay down next to her sister.

Clint started first with Elena, running his mouth over her while moving his hands over her sister, and then reversing the process.

Following that he nestled his face in Elena's crotch, his tongue and mouth busily working on her, his right hand rubbing and probing Maria's pussy. Both women were moaning and lifting their hips, and eventually he changed places. He found it odd—but maybe not, since they were sisters—to find that both women tasted exactly the same.

When he had satisfied Maria, he mounted Elena, driving himself into her, and this time he gave his attention to only the one woman. Maria got on her knees and pressed herself to the back of him, caressing his buttocks and occasionally reaching between them to fondle his testicles.

When it was Maria's turn, she insisted on getting on all fours, so he got on his knees behind her, took hold of her hips, and drove himself into her. She gasped and almost screamed, her entire body tensing, and then she relaxed and began moving against him. Elena watched, at first, then came to Clint and kissed him, first his mouth, then his neck, his shoulders, his chest, his back while he continued to drive in and out of her sister. . . .

Sometime later he did allow the sisters to take command, lying on his back while they roamed his body with hands, mouths, tongues, teasing him, sucking him, biting him. He watched them, admiring the firmness of their bodies, which seemed to be without any excess flesh at all. Their breasts were small, but their nipples were large and brown and extremely sensitive. He swore at one point that while rubbing her nipples over the hair on his legs Maria shuddered in orgasm.

They turned him over and covered his buttocks and thighs with kisses. Finally he turned over and they took turns squatting on his cock, riding him, driving him to the brink and then switching, and then somehow deciding between them which of them would remain on him when he exploded inside her. And to tell the truth, at that point he really didn't know which one of them it was. . . .

Later, lying on the bed almost exhausted, he watched them dress in silence, both looking very satisfied with themselves. Before they left they both went to the bed and kissed him tenderly, then departed without another word.

Clint fell asleep with the identical scent of both sisters on the sheets and pillows to keep him company.

# SEVENTEEN

When Clint woke the next morning, he still had not recovered from the two sisters. They were every bit as acrobatic in bed as they had been on the trapeze.

He got out of bed and staggered on weakened, rubbery legs. A concession to getting older, he thought. Only a twenty-year-old could fuck all night and still walk straight in the morning.

He walked to the window and stared out. There was no doubt in his mind that Fletcher Flora had sent the sisters to him, but for what reason? To make sure he'd be interested in staying? Hell, his curiosity was already enough to do that. He would have stayed even if the sisters hadn't come to his room.

Of course, he had enjoyed spending part of

the night with Elena and Maria, but in the long run he would have liked to spend more time with the blonde, Marthayn.

He stretched, his arms high over his head, until he felt some of the kinks in his back give, then turned and looked around for his clothes. Before donning them he washed in a basin on top of the chest of drawers. Once he was dressed he realized he was hungry, too hungry to go any further than the hotel dining room.

Christian Wayne entered the bank one hour earlier than anyone else, as was his custom. It was a ten-year custom, one he had been following since he became bank manager. In all those years his bank employees had been coming to work on time inspired, he believed, by his example.

Wayne enjoyed being in the bank when no one else was there. It was quiet, peaceful—a peacefulness that he didn't get at home. His wife, Agatha—to whom he had been married for twenty-six years, God only knew how—kept her mouth going from the time she got up until the time he left for work, and probably the rest of the day. All he knew was that when he got back home her mouth was still going—which was why he often worked late.

Wayne walked into his office and put his genuine leather briefcase on top of his desk. He rubbed his hand over the leather. He had bought the case just last year, on the tenth anniversary of his being named manager of the bank. People in town would laugh if they knew that the case was more often than not empty, but that didn't matter to him.

Christian Wayne was about to sit at his desk when he suddenly noticed something. He didn't know what it was, but something just didn't feel right to him. This was his bank, and he knew when things weren't right.

He walked out into the bank again, leaving his office door open, and looked around. What he saw widened his eyes, and sent him running for the sheriff.

Sheriff Abner Goodman followed the jabbering manager into the bank. Goodman swore that Christian Wayne sounded just like his wife at that moment. Wayne's wife was known to have the fastest mouth in town, but right now Wayne's mouth was going twice as fast as hers ever did.

" . . . don't know how this could have happened. We have the best safe in the world. It couldn't have been opened by anyone but me . . ."

"Well," Sheriff Goodman said, staring at the open door of the walk-in safe, "it's open, sure as I'm standing here."

"Yes, it is," Wayne said. "That's what I've been telling you. It's open, and the only way it could have been opened is by . . . by . . . magic."

"Magic, huh?" Sheriff Goodman said, rubbing his jaw. The lawman had been one of the crowd watching the Great Matthew perform his magic the day before at the carnival. He knew a lot of people who swore that the man had done real magic. The sheriff himself, he was sort of on the fence about it.

"Are you sure?"

"I'm sure," Wayne said, agitated, "I'm damned sure. That safe could not have been opened any other way by anyone but me."

"Magic, huh?" the sheriff said again.

# EIGHTEEN

After breakfast Clint came out of the hotel in time to see the sheriff following an agitated man across the street to the bank. Moments later a crowd was gathering in front of the bank, and he went over to see what was going on.

" . . . our money," someone was saying as he approached, "and it's all gone."

"Oh my God!" a woman shouted. "All our money?"

After that people just started shouting.

"What do we do?"

"Who did it?"

"Did anybody see them?"

"I didn't hear no shootin'!"

"When did they do it?"

At that moment the sheriff and the other

man—Clint assumed he was the bank manager—came out to face the crowd and tell them the story.

The sheriff raised his hands for the crowd to settle down.

"What happened, Sheriff?" someone demanded.

"Where's our money?"

"Who took it?"

"If you'll all be quiet, I'll tell you what we know," the sheriff announced.

He waited a few moments for the last few shouts to die down.

"Now all we know is that sometime during the night somebody broke into the bank, got into the safe, and took out all the money."

"What do ya mean, that's all you know?" someone called out.

"The money's gone, Ned," the sheriff said. "We don't know who took it, or how they got in and out."

"I thought we had a newfangled bank vault, Christian," the man named Ned called.

"The safe was opened somehow," the bank manager said, mopping his brow. "As bank manager, I should have been the only one who could open it."

"Then how was it opened?"

The bank manager spread his hands in a helpless gesture and stammered, "I don't . . . I mean, it had to be . . . it must have been . . . magic!"

"Magic?" Ned yelled.

"Hey," another voice said, "that carnival's got a magician. Maybe he did it."

"You're crazy," Ned said. "He can't do real magic."

"It looked like real magic to me," the other man said.

"You're crazy, Roy."

"Well, my money's gone, Ned, and so is yours," Roy said. "You want it back or not?"

"Damn right I want it back."

"Then we got to try anything we can," Roy said. "Sheriff, you gonna question that magician?"

"Hell," still another man said, "we should be talkin' to that whole freaky carnival bunch."

"Yeah," someone called out, "I'll talk to the two high-flyin' ladies, huh?"

"Let's get a posse together!" Roy called out.

Clint watched the sheriff to see how he was going to handle this. He had the potential for a real problem on his hands.

"Okay, settle down," the lawman shouted, but nobody was listening. They were already counting heads for a posse.

The man named Roy turned to Clint and said, "What about it, mister?"

"What about what?"

"You ridin' with the posse?"

"I don't have any money in your bank."

"Yeah, well, right now neither do I."

"I think you better listen to your sheriff."

Roy turned around to look at Goodman just

as the sheriff drew his gun, pointed it at the sky, and pulled the trigger. That got everybody's attention.

"Now listen up," the sheriff said. "Nobody's going anywhere until I say so."

"And when's that gonna be?" Ned asked.

"When I say so, Ned," Goodman said, holstering his gun. "Not before."

"So what are you gonna do?" Roy asked.

"My job, Roy," Goodman said. "My job. Now I want all of you to go home."

"Sheriff—" Ned started.

"Now!" Goodman said. "Go home!"

Slowly, the crowd began to disperse. Clint looked at the sheriff with renewed respect.

As the people moved away, Clint stood where he was and eventually Goodman saw him there. He turned and said something to the bank manager, who shook his head and went inside. Goodman came down off the boardwalk and approached Clint.

"Did you hear?"

"I heard."

"Can you help?"

"With what?"

"The carnival people."

"What about them?"

"You heard these folks, didn't you?" Goodman said. "They think the carnival people had something to do with this bank robbery."

"So?"

"What can you tell me?"

"Nothing."

"Come on," Goodman said. "I saw you talking to their leader."

"Fletcher Flora."

Goodman shook his head. "What a name. Yeah, that's him. He came to talk to me about putting his little show on. You think he had anything to do with the bank?"

"How would I know that?"

"You're friends."

"I met him the day before you did," Clint said. "That doesn't make us friends."

"That's not the way it looks to me."

"Sheriff," Clint said, "I can't help the way it looks to you."

Goodman stared at him for a few moments, then said, "All right, then I'm asking you to help me."

"How?"

"I want to talk to this fella, Fletcher."

"So talk to him."

"I want you to take me to their camp," Goodman said. "I want to talk to him out there."

"Why do you need me?"

"Maybe he'll talk to me easier with you along," Goodman said.

"Maybe not."

"Well, we won't know until we try, will we?" Goodman asked.

"What do you think, Sheriff?"

"About what?"

"About the bank vault," Clint said. "You think it was opened by magic?"

"Magic," Goodman said, rubbing his hand over his face. "Was that guy really doing magic yesterday?"

"I don't know."

"Well, I don't know how that vault was opened," Goodman said. "Maybe it was magic, and maybe it wasn't. All I know is I got to do my job, and that means asking some questions. I'm asking you to help me."

"Sure," Clint said. "Why not?"

"All right," Goodman said, "thanks."

"But all I'm going to do is take you out there. You do all the talking. Agreed?"

"Agreed."

"All right, then," Clint said. "When do you want to go?"

"How about now?"

# NINETEEN

When Marthayn heard that the Great Matthew had asked for her, she sat in her tent for a few moments. It didn't take the ability to tell the future for her to know what he wanted. Since the day he'd arrived he had made it clear that he had taken a liking to her. Since then he had called for her half a dozen times, and always for the same thing. Fletcher had made it clear to her that she didn't have a choice.

"It will only be until we can figure out a way to get rid of him," Fletcher had told her.

"So I'm a whore until that time, right?" Marthayn had asked.

"Don't put it that way," he had said.

This morning Fletcher had come to her tent and simply told her, "He wants you."

She had glared at him and said, "Get out."
Fletcher had turned and left.

After Fletcher left her tent, Marthayn stood
up and trudged over to Matthew's wagon. She
was about to knock on the door when it suddenly opened, as if by itself.

"Come in," Matthew's voice said.

She entered the wagon and couldn't see anything, it was so dark—but that was usually the
case. Since his arrival the only time anyone
ever really saw Matthew was when he was performing. She probably got closer to him than
anyone else, but it was always in the dark—
and it was usually so dark that there was not
even any night vision. She felt Matthew, felt
him touch her, felt him lie on top of her, felt
him enter her, but she never saw him.

She wondered idly, as he undressed her, if
he ever felt her shudder.

# TWENTY

As Clint and Sheriff Abner Goodman approached the carnival, Clint noticed how still the place was. It appeared that carnies might not be early risers.

He realized how wrong he was when Fletcher Flora stepped into view just as they rode up.

"Morning, Fletcher."

"Clint," Fletcher said. "You're a little early for the show today. Good morning, Sheriff."

"Mr. Flora," the sheriff said. "Mind if we stand down and have a talk?"

"Suit yourself," Fletcher said. "In a few minutes I might be able to offer you some coffee."

"That's okay," the sheriff said, dismounting. Clint dismounted just behind him.

"We'd like to talk—" the sheriff started, but Clint stopped him.

"Wrong, Sheriff."

"Okay," Goodman said, with a nod to Clint, "*I* want to talk to you about something that happened in town last night."

At that moment Frank Flora came into view and joined the group.

"Sheriff, this is my brother, Frank," Fletcher said, making the introductions.

"Hello," Goodman said.

"What did you want to talk to me about, Sheriff?" Fletcher asked. "Something in town, you said?"

"Yes," the lawman said. "Apparently some-one robbed the bank overnight."

Fletcher felt Frank go tense and, without the lawman seeing, put his hand against the small of his younger brother's back to steady him.

"Sheriff," Fletcher said, "every time we stop someplace to put on a performance we're blamed for everything that happens."

"I'm not blaming you—"

"Then why are you here?"

"I'm just here to ask questions—"

"Have you already questioned everyone in your town?" Fletcher asked.

"Well, no—"

"Don't you think you should have done that before coming out here?"

"Look, it doesn't matter what I do first—"

"What's your part in this, Clint?"

"I don't have a part," Clint said. "The sheriff just asked me to ride out with him."

"Like a bodyguard?"

Clint just shrugged.

"Did you think you would be harmed out here?"

The sheriff seemed to realize that he was being put on the defensive.

"Look, friend, you're in my jurisdiction now. I'm here to ask the questions."

"All right, then," Fletcher said, "go ahead and ask your questions."

"All right, then—"

"Or maybe I can save you the trouble," Fletcher said. "No one from my carnival had anything to do with robbing your bank."

"How do you know that?"

"I know my people."

"You know them that well?"

"Yes."

"But—"

"I tell you what, Sheriff," Fletcher said, "why don't you just spend some time out here and talk to my people? They should all be getting up about now. Speak to them with my blessings."

Goodman seemed to think about that.

"Could be out here all day, Sheriff," Clint said.

"Hmm," Goodman said, "I know. . . ."

"Maybe," Clint said, "somebody in town did see something."

"He won't know that unless he questions people in town," Fletcher said.

"Maybe not," Clint agreed.

Goodman looked confused.

"What do you want to do, Sheriff?" Clint asked.

Goodman started to look even more confused.

"You're a fast talker, Mr. Flora," he said finally.

"Sheriff," Fletcher said, "I just don't like it when folks blame carnival people for everything."

"I'm going to go back to town and get my deputies," Goodman said. "We'll be back to question your people, and it won't take all day."

"That's fine with us, Sheriff."

Goodman turned to mount his horse.

"Are you coming, Adams?"

"I don't think so, Sheriff," Clint said. "I'll stay around for a cup of that coffee."

Goodman nodded, mounted up, and looked down at Fletcher Flora.

"If you pull up stakes I'll know you're guilty, and I'll come after you with a posse."

"Understood, Sheriff."

Goodman gave the man one last hard look to bring his point across, then tossed a glance at Clint before turning his horse and heading back to town.

# TWENTY-ONE

After the sheriff left, Clint walked over to Fletcher and Frank Flora, trailing Duke behind him.

"What about that coffee?"

Fletcher looked at him.

"What do you want?" he asked.

"I thought the question was what you wanted," Clint said.

"Do you think one of my people robbed that bank?" the carnival boss asked.

"I don't know," Clint said. "It could have been anybody."

Fletcher looked at Frank, who gave no indication that he even knew what was going on. No expression at all crossed his face.

"All right," Fletcher said, "let's go and have that coffee."

Frank surprised Clint by putting his hand out for Duke's reins.

"Watch him," Clint said, handing the reins over, "he'll take your hand off if you're not careful."

"Frank knows how to handle horses, Clint," Fletcher said.

"I hope so."

He watched the mute man walk away with the big gelding, who followed along, surprisingly docile.

"How about that coffee?" Fletcher asked.

When they both had a cup of coffee in hand, Fletcher asked, "Can you tell me about this bank robbery?"

"All I know is that somebody got into the bank overnight and opened a bank vault that supposedly couldn't be opened."

"Then how was it done?"

"I don't know," Clint said, "but the bank manager seems to think it could only have been done by magic."

Fletcher hesitated a moment then said, "Now I see why the sheriff rode out here—Matthew."

"I guess so," Clint said. "Could he have done it, Fletch?"

"You saw his performance yesterday, Clint," Fletcher said. "If anyone could have done it, he could."

"With magic?"

Fletcher shrugged. "We talked about this yesterday," the man said. "I don't know how he does the things he does, Clint."

"Come on, Fletch," Clint said. "Real magic?"

"I've been with the carnival a lot of years," Fletcher said. "I grew up with these kinds of people, and I've hired many of them. They're all strange in their own ways. You may not believe it, but I actually do think that Marthayn can see the future."

Clint thought about her prediction that he would meet a tall, dark man. Could that be Matthew? And was that a prediction, or was he being set up?

"I don't believe it," Clint said firmly, "and I don't believe in real magic, either."

"Then how was that bank vault opened?" Fletcher asked.

"I don't know," Clint said, "and I'm not going to worry about it. That's the sheriff's job. I've got one question to ask you, though."

"What's that?"

"Are you sure about your people?"

"My people are not thieves, Clint," Fletcher said hotly. "Most of them have been with me for years. In fact, all of them have . . . except Matthew."

"I think I'd like to meet this Matthew," Clint said.

"He won't see you."

"Let's try," Clint said. "What have we got to lose?"

"Well . . . if we go over to his wagon now, we'll interrupt him."

"His sleep?"

Fletcher looked away and said, "No."

"You mean he's got a woman with him?" Clint asked. "Well, maybe she knows something about him that you don't. Have you asked her?"

"If anyone could know anything about him, it would be her," Fletcher said, "and yet she doesn't."

Clint frowned.

"Who are we talking about?"

"I think you know."

"Marthayn?"

Fletcher nodded.

"Didn't you tell me you were once involved with her?" Clint asked.

"You don't understand."

"I guess I don't." Clint dumped the remnants of his coffee on the ground and said, "Take me to his wagon."

Fletcher stared at him for a few moments, and once again Clint saw that the man was afraid of Matthew.

"All right," he said finally, "let's go."

# TWENTY-TWO

Clint followed Fletcher Flora over to the wagon that had THE GREAT MATTHEW painted on
its side. Matthew really seemed to have the
carnival boss under his thumb; Fletcher was
obviously struggling not to show his anxiety as
they drew closer to the wagon.

It seemed the other carnies were afraid of
him too, apparently because they thought he
had real magic at his command. If this was
not the case—and to Clint's mind it surely was
not—then the man had everyone cowed by the
sheer force of his ability to make them believe
in his power.

Clint wasn't anticipating being intimidated
himself.

A question came to mind, though. Did Matthew control the people enough to have them

commit robberies for him?

As they approached the wagon, Clint saw that it was closed up tight.

"Is she still in there?" he asked Fletcher.

"Probably."

Clint walked to the wagon and pounded on the door.

"Who is it?" a voice called out after a moment.

"Clint Adams."

"Who the hell are you?"

Before he could answer he heard an exchange of voices inside, a man's and a woman's.

"Go away," the man's voice called after a few moments.

"I've got some questions to ask you, Matthew," Clint called out.

"Go away."

Clint started pounding on the door again.

"You're going to get him mad," Fletcher said, but the tone of his voice indicated that he was more interested than scared at the moment.

Clint continued to pound.

Finally, the door was opened and Marthayn stood there. Her clothes were on, but she was disheveled. Her eyes, as she stared at Clint, appeared dead.

"Clint," she said, "you better go away."

"Come out here, Marthayn," Clint said.

"I . . . can't."

One of her arms was out of sight behind the door, and Clint instinctively knew that Matthew had ahold of it.

"Come on," he said gently, reaching out for her. "You're finished here."

"Go away," he heard Matthew's voice call.

"Matthew, come on out," Clint said. "I want to ask you some questions."

"About what?"

"About a bank robbery in town."

The man's voice was not deep, but it was steady, strong. Clint wondered why he didn't use it at all during his act.

"I don't know nothin' about a bank robbery."

"Step out where I can see you."

"Go away," the voice said again, "before you make me angry."

"I have no problem with making you angry, mister," Clint said. "I'm not afraid of you like these other people are."

"Clint—"

"I don't believe in magic," Clint added.

There was a moment of silence and then Matthew's voice said ominously, "I could make you believe."

"No," Clint said, "I don't think you could."

Abruptly he took hold of Marthayn's loose arm and yanked on it, pulling her out the door. He thought he heard something strike the door, and then a muffled cry of pain. Maybe he'd dislocated the magician's arm. Too bad.

Marthayn almost tumbled down the steps but he caught her weight and lowered her to the ground gently.

"You can go back to your tent," Clint said.

She brushed back an errant lock of hair, glared at Fletcher, and then walked away.

As Clint looked up at the wagon door it slammed shut.

"I don't think he's coming out," Fletcher said.

Clint debated for a moment the wisdom of kicking the door in, but he had no right, no authority. Leave that to the sheriff.

"The sheriff will be back later to question him, and then he'll have to open it."

"I'm not so sure about that."

Clint turned to the man.

"What kind of hold does he have over you, Fletch? Over the rest of these people?"

Fletcher didn't answer.

"Is it fear, pure and simple?" Clint went on. "Is that it? Fear of his . . . his magic?"

"You've seen him work, Clint—"

"I don't believe in magic, Fletch!" Clint said, cutting the man off. "He does what he does by the use of tricks of some sort. He's not some . . . some magical being."

Fletcher gave Clint a doubtful look and said, "You'd have to prove that to a lot of the people around here."

"You included?"

Again the man didn't answer.

"Well," Clint said, "we'll see. I'll be back later to see today's performance."

Fletcher nodded and said, "I'll have Frank bring your horse around."

## TWENTY-THREE

After Clint left, Fletcher debated going to talk to Matthew, but he was sure the man would send for him soon enough. Instead he decided to go and see Marthayn.

When he got to her tent, she had straightened her clothes and fixed her hair.

"What was that all about?" she asked him.

"Just what we wanted it to be about," Fletcher said. "Clint Adams is interested in you, he's interested in Matthew, and I think he's pretty much involved with this now."

"So you think he's going to get rid of Matthew for you?"

"I hope so."

"Because you and your brother can't do it for yourselves?"

He firmed his jaw and said, "We've already

had this talk, Marthayn."

"I don't see why you have to have someone do your dirty work for you, Fletch. You and Frank and some of the others ought to be able to run Matthew off."

"None of the others are willing to try it," he said. "They're scared."

"And you?"

He hesitated, then said, "I'm careful."

"And Frank?"

"He just does what I tell him."

"Then tell him to face Matthew and get rid of him," she said.

Fletcher said nothing.

"You're afraid," she said. "Afraid that Matthew has some magical power that he'll use to kill you, or your brother."

"Do you think you're telling me something that I don't know?" Fletcher demanded angrily. "What about you? Why do you go to him and let him do what he wants to do?"

Now it was her turn to be silent.

"What happened this morning?" he asked, his tone more gentle.

"Nothing," she said. "Clint Adams got there before anything could happen."

"Then he's going to want you again."

"I don't think so."

"Why not?"

"Because I think Clint hurt his arm."

"Oh, great," Fletcher said. "If he's hurt, he won't be able to perform today."

"Now you're worried about your business?"

she asked. "If he's hurt, then maybe he's not this magical person everyone thinks he is. How about that?"

Fletcher thought about that for a few moments and then said, "Maybe I ought to find out."

"Maybe you should," she said.

He hesitated a moment, then backed out through the tent flap.

Marthayn sat down and stared at her crystal ball. If only the thing really could tell her the future, but it couldn't, any more than the Great Matthew could perform feats of magic. Why then did the entire carnival company allow him to control them so?

She knew that her ability to predict the future was a sham, so she assumed that Matthew's magic powers were also fake . . .

But what if they weren't?

What if what Matthew did really was magic, and Fletcher and Frank and everyone else were right to fear him?

That meant the only person who wasn't afraid to stand up to him was Clint Adams. Which meant it was going to be up to Clint to get rid of him. If he didn't, Marthayn didn't know what she would do, because she had no intention of ever going back to Matthew's wagon.

Ever.

# TWENTY-FOUR

Fletcher Flora was of two minds. He truly wanted to be rid of Matthew, but he also wanted the man to perform today. The last thing he needed was for people to come to see the magician and have him be unable to do his act.

On the other hand, in light of the bank robbery, were people going to come at all?

He got to Matthew's wagon and knocked on the door.

"Go away," the magician's voice called out.

"Matthew, it's me, Fletcher."

"Go away."

"Matthew, I have to know if you're going to be able to do your act today."

There was a long silence, and then Matthew

said, "No. That man hurt my arm. Who was he?"

The man's voice sounded petulant, like a small child's tone when something is going on that the child just can't understand.

"His name is Clint Adams."

Pause.

"Why do I know that name?"

"He's a very famous gunman known as the Gunsmith," Fletcher said. Maybe this information alone would scare the magician away.

"Why was he here?"

Fletcher hesitated a moment, then said, "To see Marthayn." He let that sink in, then added, "And to ask questions about a bank robbery."

There was another long pause.

"Would you know anything about that, Matthew?"

Pause.

"I don't know about any bank robbery," Matthew said, "and I can't perform today. You'll have to replace me with someone else."

"Like who?"

There was absolutely no pause this time, which should have told Fletcher something right away.

"What about your friend, the gunman?" Matthew asked. "If he's so good with a gun, make him perform."

"I don't think he'll do it."

"Sure he will," Matthew's voice said from the confines of his wagon. "After all, isn't he the one who hurt me? It's his fault I can't go on, and it'll be his fault if you lose money."

Fletcher thought that over. It made sense, and if Clint would do it, it would be a fabulous attraction: The Gunsmith doing trick shooting!

"Ask him," Matthew called out. "He'll do it. Or have Marthayn ask him."

Fletcher backed away from the wagon, then felt he should say something.

"I'll ask him and see what he says."

Silence.

"Do you need anything?"

No answer.

"Matthew?"

Still nothing.

"All right," Fletcher said and backed away from the wagon.

He turned when he was a few hundred feet from it and started walking quickly. Coming toward him he saw his brother.

"Matthew's arm is hurt and he can't perform," Fletcher told him.

Frank shrugged.

"We need a replacement."

Frank raised his eyebrows as if to ask who.

"Clint Adams," Fletcher said. "Get me a horse. I'm going to ride into town and ask him."

Frank made a rubbing motion with the first three fingers of his right hand.

"Yes, we'll make money off of it."

Frank nodded and duplicated the move.

"Oh, the bank robbery?"

Frank nodded.

"Matthew says he knows nothing about it."

Frank frowned and looked questioningly at his brother.

"Do I believe him? Hell, I don't know, and I'm not going to think about it. In fact, I don't care whether he did it or not. All I care about is getting Adams into a situation where he'll face Matthew. We'll see which wins out, magic or a bullet."

Frank stroked his jaw to show that he was thinking about it.

"We'll find out soon enough," Fletcher said. "Saddle my horse. I want to go into town as soon as possible."

Frank touched his chest, where a sheriff's badge would be if he had one.

"I don't know about the sheriff," Fletcher said. "If he comes back, it'll be to ask questions. We'll worry about that when the time comes."

Frank had more questions, but Fletcher waved them away with his hands.

"Go and get my horse for me now, Frank," he said. "Do it."

Frank nodded and went off to saddle his brother's horse.

# TWENTY-FIVE

When Clint got back to Benton's Fork, he returned Duke to the livery stable and walked to the sheriff's office. The door was locked and when he knocked there was no answer. Apparently, the sheriff was out doing his job, investigating the robbery.

He walked over to the bank just out of curiosity and found that it was open for business. He walked inside and immediately saw the door of the safe that had been opened by some sort of "magic." It was a huge metal door the like of which Clint had never seen before. He wondered how anyone would be able to open it without the combination.

Magic?

No.

"Can I help you, sir?" an older woman asked him.

"No," Clint said, "I was just looking."

He left the teller standing there with a puzzled expression on her face and went back outside.

It was still early enough to have a late breakfast so Clint walked back to his hotel to eat in the dining room.

Clint was halfway through his ham and eggs and potatoes when he spotted Fletcher Flora entering the dining room. The man looked around the room, saw Clint, and started walking toward his table.

Flora was about halfway across the room when somebody reached out and grabbed his arm.

"You got some nerve comin' into this town," a man said aloud, attracting the attention of all the other diners in the room. The man was glaring intently at the carnival boss.

. The man who was speaking was sitting at a table with another man, who was also giving Fletcher Flora some bad looks.

"I don't know what you mean," Flora said, pulling his arm away. "Excuse me."

"Don't walk away from me, you freak keeper," the man yelled, standing up.

Clint saw Fletcher stiffen and turn. The man he was facing was bigger by several inches and carried a lot more weight, although much of it was gut. Still, the man looked like a mean customer.

"What did you call me?"

The man could see that he had gotten to Fletcher Flora with the remark, so he smiled.

"Freak keeper," the man said, "that's what I called you. You got a bunch of freaks out there and we think that you and your freaks robbed our bank."

"Bank robbing freaks," the man seated at the table contributed.

"What do ya got to say about that, freak keeper?" the first man asked, jabbing his finger into Fletcher's chest.

Fletcher didn't answer with words. Almost faster than Clint could follow, Fletcher hit the other man three times, twice in the stomach and once on the point of the jaw. The bigger man stiffened and went down like he'd been poleaxed.

His friend watched him fall, then stood up before he could think twice about it. He too was bigger than Fletcher.

"Hey—" he said, but he had no time to get anything else said or done.

Fletcher swung one more time, hitting this man once with a roundhouse right and knocking him to the floor.

That done he turned and walked to Clint's table.

# TWENTY-SIX

"May I sit down?" Fletcher asked.

Clint looked past Fletcher to where the two men he had hit were still lying on the floor. Fletcher turned and looked as well.

"I usually control my temper better than that," he said to Clint.

"You hit hard."

"I started out as a fighter with the carnival," Fletcher explained. "The carnival paid anyone who could last three rounds with me."

"Did anyone ever get paid?"

"No," Fletcher said, "but I was heavier then."

"Well, have a seat and I'll get you some coffee," Clint said. "Hopefully, we won't be interrupted by the sheriff."

"Everyone heard him insult me," Fletcher said, sitting opposite Clint. "I was justified."

"I, uh, wouldn't argue that point with you," Clint said.

The waiter, seeing Fletcher sit, brought over another cup, and Clint waved him away and filled it.

"I get the feeling that when you walked in here you were looking for me."

"You're right, I was."

"Was there something we didn't talk about this morning?" Clint asked.

"Something I didn't know about, yes." Fletcher picked up his cup and took a sip of coffee, then made a face and put it down. "The coffee at our camp is better."

"I agree," Clint said. "What did you want to talk to me about?"

"Matthew."

"What about him?"

"He's hurt."

"What?"

"You hurt him this morning," Fletcher said. "He can't perform."

Clint hesitated then asked, "What is that supposed to mean to me?"

Fletcher leaned forward.

"I need you."

"To do what?" Clint asked. "Talk to Matthew again? You want me to apologize?"

"No, nothing like that," Fletcher said.

"Then what?"

"I need you to perform."

"What?"

"I need you to replace Matthew—"

"I don't know any magic tricks, Fletcher," Clint said. "What do you expect me to do?"

"What you do best," Fletcher said, "shoot."

"Oh no," Clint said. "I'm not a trick shooter for hire, Fletcher."

"I am not trying to hire you," the man said.

"You're not?"

"No," Fletcher said, "I am not offering to pay you."

Clint narrowed his eyes and stared across the table at him. Behind Fletcher the two men were getting to their feet. The first one seemed to want to try Fletcher again, but the second one had other ideas and pulled his friend from the room.

"You're serious, aren't you?"

"Very."

"You want me to replace Matthew, do some trick shooting, and do it for free?"

"Yes."

"And you think this is a reasonable request?"

"Considering you're the one that injured him."

"How do I know that?"

Fletcher smiled and said, "I'm telling you. You did it this morning when you barged in on him and Marthayn."

"Barged in?"

"What would you call it?"

Clint opened his mouth, then closed it. What did he call it? He had barged in on them, but even now he felt justified in having done so.

"Okay, how badly is he hurt?"

"I don't know," Fletcher said. "Are you going to eat that piece of ham?"

Clint looked down at the piece of ham in question and said, "No. Go ahead."

Fletcher reached across the table and plucked the ham from Clint's plate.

"Your friends have left."

"Hmm?" Fletcher said. "My friends?"

Clint pointed behind him. Fletcher looked and realized that the two men he had fought with were gone.

"They might be waiting for you outside," Clint said. "I'd better leave with you."

"Leave?" Fletcher asked, chewing on the ham. "I'm not leaving until I know that you'll replace Matthew."

"For how long?"

"Just for today," Fletcher said. "I already have a show planned and I have to fill his spot."

"And tomorrow?"

"Tomorrow's my problem," Fletcher said. "I just need you for today."

Clint thought it over. It was true that he had injured Matthew, and he felt badly about that. What would it hurt to help Fletcher out just for one afternoon?

"All right."

"You'll do it?"

"Yes," Clint said, "I'll do it. What time do you want me?"

"One o'clock, so we'll be ready by three. What will you require?"

"Require?" Clint thought a moment. "Just my guns, and some targets, I guess."

"All right. We can talk about what kind of targets you want this afternoon."

"Fine. Come on, I'll walk you out."

"I can go out by myself, Clint," Fletcher said. "I can take care of myself."

"I know that," Clint said. "I saw you do it, but you don't have a gun, and next time they may not want to fight fair."

Fletcher frowned and said, "You have a point. Maybe walking out with you isn't such a bad idea."

They walked out of the dining room and out of the hotel together.

"Yours?" Clint asked, pointing to the horse tied in front of the hotel.

"Yes."

"Well, it looks like your friends had enough the first time," Clint said.

"I'll get back to the camp, then," Fletcher said. "I'll have to get something set up for you. One o'clock, right, Clint?"

"One o'clock. I'll be there."

"Good."

As Fletcher walked to his horse, Clint thought of something else.

"Fletch?"

"Yes?"

"There is something else I'll need."

"What's that?"

"An assistant."

"I'll have a man assist—"

"No, not a man," Clint said, "a woman."

"Maria? Elena?"

"No," Clint said, "neither of them. I want Marthayn to be my assistant."

"Marthayn?" Fletcher said, and then he smiled. "I understand, Clint. Marthayn will be there to assist you."

"Okay."

Clint watched the man mount up rather inexpertly and ride out of town. After that he went upstairs to clean his gun. If he was going to perform, he wanted to make sure his equipment was in proper working order.

# TWENTY-SEVEN

Before leaving town Clint went over to the sheriff's office to talk to the man about the robbery.

"Sheriff Goodman," Clint said, as he walked into the office.

Goodman looked up and made a face. He wasn't happy to see Clint.

"What is it, Mr. Adams? I'm very busy."

"Working on the robbery?"

"Yes," Goodman said, "working on the robbery."

"Did you find any witnesses in town?"

"No, no witnesses."

"Well, what's your next move?"

Sheriff Goodman heaved a great sigh.

"I'm going back out to the carnival to question those people."

"Sheriff, you suspect them just because they're strangers?"

"That's right."

"Do you suspect me because I'm a stranger also?"

Goodman looked alarmed that Clint Adams—the Gunsmith—might think he suspected him of something.

"No, Adams," Goodman said. "I don't suspect you."

"All right, then," Clint said. "Are you going out to the carnival this afternoon?"

"Yes, I am," Goodman said. "Me and my deputies, we're gonna question those carnival . . . freaks."

Clint remembered what Fletcher Flora had done to the last man who'd used the word "freak."

"Sheriff, a piece of advice."

"What's that?"

"When you go out there today," Clint said, "don't use that word."

"What word?"

"Freak."

"Why not?"

"They don't like it."

Goodman seemed to be thinking it over.

"Take my advice, Sheriff," Clint said, and headed for the door.

"Adams?"

"Yeah?"

"You gonna be out there today?"

"Oh yeah," Clint said, "I'll be out there."

• • •

Outside Clint climbed astride Duke and headed out to the carnival grounds. He wondered what was going to happen tomorrow, after he did his performance, after Sheriff Goodman questioned everyone. Would the carnival move on, still in the hold of the magician, Matthew? Or would the sheriff find out something that would cause him to hold them here?

Since he was going out there anyway, Clint thought maybe he'd ask a few questions of his own.

# TWENTY-EIGHT

By the time Clint arrived at the carnival camp, everyone knew that he would be performing in place of the Great Matthew. He was met with enthusiasm, as the carnival had never had such a famous personality on the bill before.

Frank took Duke from him and walked him off. Clint was once again surprised at how easily the big gelding went with the silent man. He wondered if the fact that Frank was mute might have had something to do with it.

"Clint," Fletcher called, hurrying over to greet him.

"Fletcher," Clint said. "I see the news has gotten around."

"Everyone is very excited about it."

"Why?" Clint said. "It's not as if I can do

117

something extraordinary, like some of your people."

"I guess we'll see whether you can or not," Fletcher said. "Are you ready?"

"I'd like to see my assistant first," Clint said. "Has she agreed?"

"Oh yes," Fletcher said, "she agreed. Come on, we'll go to her tent."

In point of fact Marthayn had not so much agreed to be Clint's assistant as she had been ordered by Fletcher to do so.

"Why do you keep pushing me on this man?" Marthayn asked. "Can't Maria and Elena handle him?"

"He's not interested in Maria and Elena," Fletcher said, "he's interested in you. You'll assist him in his act."

"Doing what?"

Fletcher had spread his hands and said, "Whatever he wants you to do."

Marthayn put her hands on her hips.

"And how is this going to help us, Fletcher?" she asked. "How is this going to get rid of Matthew for us?"

"I don't know yet," Fletcher said. "But at least it gets Adams out here. Don't resist me on this, Marthayn."

"Resisting is something I should start doing," Marthayn said, "and I will, if this doesn't work."

"You'll resist Matthew?"

"Matthew, you, everyone," Marthayn said.

"I'll go off on my own, Fletch."

"You'd leave the carnival?"

"I'd leave *this* carnival," she said, "and be glad to leave it behind."

Fletcher stared at her.

"I can't believe you'd do that."

"I guess we'll just have to wait and see, Fletch," she said. "When Clint Adams gets here, bring him over."

Fletcher led Clint to Marthayn's tent and said, "I'll stay out here."

"She's mad at you, huh?"

Fletcher's mouth twitched and he said, "She's always mad at me."

Clint approached the entrance to the tent, but before he could say anything he heard her call out, "You can come in, Clint."

He entered the tent and found her sitting at that little table with the big crystal ball in the center of it. She was wearing a blouse that showed her shoulders, but her hair was down, covering her somewhat.

"I understand I'm to be your assistant in your act," she said.

"My act," Clint repeated. He hadn't thought of it that way yet, but he guessed she was right. "That's right. I need an assistant. You know, someone to hold up the cards, keep a cigarette in her mouth—"

"I don't smoke."

"Then you won't have to light the thing," he said, "will you?"

Marthayn stared at him for a few moments and then asked, "You're not kidding, are you?"

"Yes," he said, "I am."

"No cigarettes?"

"No cigarettes."

Marthayn seemed visibly relieved.

"What will I have to do, then?"

"I don't know," he said, with a shrug. "I don't know yet what I'm going to do."

"Haven't you done this before?"

"No."

"You've never performed before?"

"No," he said. "Why?"

"It's just that you have the . . . the demeanor of a showman."

"Really?"

She smiled and said, "Yes, really."

"Well," he said, "maybe you and your crystal ball there can tell me what my . . . my act is going to be like."

"I don't need the ball," she said. "You're going to be fine."

"Fine," he said, nodding his head and scratching his nose. "That's high praise, huh?"

She stood up and said, "From me it is."

He saw that she was wearing a long, billowy skirt of some gauzy fabric.

"Come on," she said, "we'd better go and rehearse so you'll have some idea what you're going to do."

# TWENTY-NINE

In his wagon the Great Matthew flexed his arm, testing it. The pain wasn't too bad. In fact, he could have performed if he really wanted to, but he didn't want to. Let this fellow Clint Adams do it instead, and then Matthew would have an opportunity to observe the man and see what he could do.

Matthew had a storm lamp burning in the wagon, but he kept the flame very low. He did not like bright lights, which is why he rarely came out of his wagon, and why he usually performed late in the afternoon.

He prepared his own meals on a small stove inside the wagon, but he rarely ate, and when he did he ate light. He was thirty-five years old, and each year he found he could exist on less and less food. Water was the only thing he craved, and he drank gallons of it a day. There was just enough room in his wagon for him to do some exercise, so he was fit. The only other thing he needed on occasion was a woman, and that was never a problem. Whenever he called for Marthayn, she came to him. He knew she didn't come of her own free will, but that mattered little to him. Nothing much mattered to Matthew except what he wanted—and he usually got what he wanted.

He'd discovered some years ago that he had a strong will and was able to impose it on other people—usually people with little or no will of their own. His greatest triumph, to date, was his control of Fletcher Flora. Outwardly Fletcher appeared to be a very strong-willed man but soon after they met Matthew realized that he would be able to control Fletcher, if he played him right.

The other carnies were easier. All he had to do was convince them that his magic was real, and they were ready to do anything for him.

Magic, Matthew believed, was a matter of will. He was a failure until he realized that. You can make people see anything and believe anything if you can control their minds. Matthew had found a place where he not only controlled minds and wills, but he controlled these people's world.

Of late, however, he realized that they were growing restless, especially Fletcher and Marthayn.

Fletcher thought he was going to use this man Clint Adams to get rid of him. Matthew knew of Adams's reputation as the Gunsmith, but he had no intention of ever confronting Adams with a gun. Adams wasn't going to shoot down an unarmed man, was he?

Matthew doubted it.

So what could Clint Adams do to him?

Still he wanted to keep an eye on his potential adversary. The man was going to have to rehearse his "act," and the magician wanted to be able to watch him do so. There were a few places someone could rehearse an act like that, and from his vantage point he'd be able to see a couple of them. With any luck, Adams would pick one of those places.

Or perhaps Marthayn would . . . if the Great Matthew thought about it enough.

He sat down, doused the light of the lamp completely, and concentrated.

# THIRTY

"Wait," Marthayn said.

"What is it?"

She frowned, then shook her head. She had been leading him to a field east of the carnival camp, but suddenly she stopped.

"I think the other field would be better," she said.

"Which one?"

"West," she said. "West of the camp."

"All right," he said, having no preference, "lead the way."

On the way Clint spotted Fletcher and several of the carnies coming toward them carrying things they could use as targets. He pointed, and they changed direction to match them.

When they reached the field west of camp,

Clint saw that the men were carrying cans and bottles to be used as targets.

"Do you have any cards?"

"Cards?" one of the men asked.

"Playing cards?" Fletcher said. "Yes, we have cards." He took a deck from his pocket and handed it to Clint.

"Here," Clint said, handing the deck to Marthayn.

"What am I supposed to do with these?" she asked.

"Hold them."

"Huh? I thought you were kidding about that."

"No," he said, "I was kidding about the cigarette. I want you to hold the cards."

She looked down at the deck in her hand and said, "How?"

"One at a time."

She glared at him.

"Why don't we start with bottles and cans?" he suggested.

They rehearsed for an hour, and Clint thought that it was harder on Marthayn than on him. It was up to her to set up the bottles and cans, to throw them into the air one after the other. All he had to do was shatter them or puncture them with a well-placed shot.

"Don't you ever miss?" she asked him at one point.

"I hope not," he said, but the truth of the matter was that he didn't miss. He hit whatever he pointed at. To him the gun was just an extension of his finger.

At one point, while shooting at some stationary targets, Clint noticed that he could see Matthew's wagon from here. If that was the case, then Matthew was also able to see him.

"Do you think he's watching?" Fletcher asked, from behind him.

Clint turned and looked at the carny boss.

"You know him better than I do," Clint said. "You tell me."

"Oh, he's watching."

"Why?"

"He wants to see what you can do."

"Again," Clint said, "why?"

Fletcher just stared, his eyes flat and expressionless.

"What do you expect my presence to do to him, Fletch?" he asked. "Chase him off?"

"No," Fletcher said, "just your presence won't do that."

"Then what will?"

"I don't know."

"Do you expect me to get rid of him for you?"

"I expect you to do some shooting, Clint," Fletcher said. "That's all."

Now Marthayn tossed another can into the air, which Clint hit three times before it struck the ground. He turned to look at her and she returned his look expectantly.

"Okay," he said, "let's get the cards."

# THIRTY-ONE

Later Clint sat by the fire and ate some lunch with Fletcher and Marthayn. It was an odd thing to see these two together. Fletcher had indicated that he and Marthayn had had a relationship at one point, and from what Clint could see they were painfully polite to each other around him. He did not know how they acted when they were alone.

"I think what you did with the cards was . . . unbelievable," Fletcher said.

"Yes," Marthayn said, flexing her fingers as if very glad that she still had them all, "so do I."

Clint did not reply.

"What did it feel like?" Fletcher asked Marthayn. "I mean, when the bullet went through the card."

"It was odd," Marthayn said. "The bullet passed through so smoothly that I hardly felt it."

"And right through a symbol each time," Fletcher said, shaking his head.

He had the deck in his pocket and took it out now. Clint had fired at the complete deck of fifty-two cards. Fletcher looked at a few of them at random now. An ace of diamonds pierced right through the diamond. A ten of hearts pierced through the top right heart. A three of clubs with a hole punched through the center club.

"Amazing," Fletcher said, holding up another one, the three of spades, with the middle spade punched out.

"On that one," Clint said, pointing, "I was aiming for the bottom spade."

"What?" Marthayn asked, alarmed.

"He's kidding," Fletcher said. "Remember, he said he doesn't aim, he points."

Fletcher spread the cards in his hands, all neatly holed, then put them back in his pocket.

"Thank you for letting me keep these," he said to Clint.

"My pleasure," Clint said. "We'll use another deck for the show."

"So you've decided what you will do during your act?" Fletcher asked.

"I think the cans in the air . . ."

"Oh, yes!" Fletcher said.

"And the cards . . ."

"Yes," Marthayn said, nodding.

"I don't know how impressive it will be shooting at stationary targets," Clint said.

"You should do that first," Fletcher said.

"Why? There will certainly be men in the crowd who have done it themselves."

"It will lull the crowd into thinking that your act is simple, perhaps even boring."

"I see what you mean," Clint said. "All right."

"I have another suggestion, as well," Fletcher said.

"Let's hear it."

"When you are finished, we can ask if there is anyone who wants to shoot against you," Fletcher said.

"And you'll charge them?"

"A nominal free," Fletcher said. "Perhaps as little as a nickel a shot."

"And what happens if someone beats me?"

"Can someone beat you?"

"Anything's possible," Clint said. "But I doubt it."

"Then there is nothing to worry about," Fletcher said, "but we will offer some sort of prize."

"Will you do it?" Marthayn asked.

"Sure," Clint said, "why not?"

"Some of the people will pay just to say they shot against the Gunsmith."

Fletcher saw the look on Clint's face.

"It's all right for me to bill you that way, isn't it?" the carny boss asked.

"Yeah, sure," Clint said, "go ahead."

Fletcher stood up.

"I'll have to have some posters made up quickly. We don't have time to put them up in town, but we'll have them up all over the grounds."

Clint poured himself another cup of coffee.

"Get some rest, Clint," Fletcher said. "You'll go on at five, so you have over two hours."

"Right."

"Marthayn," Fletcher said, "find him someplace to lie down."

"All right."

Fletcher walked away, and Marthayn looked across the fire at Clint. Their eyes met and held, and something passed between them.

"Do you want to lie down?" she asked.

"It might not be a bad idea."

"You can use my tent, then."

He nodded.

"That doesn't sound like a bad idea, either. We can talk about the . . . act."

"Oh?" she asked. "You expect me to stay in the tent while you rest?"

"I expect you to stay in the tent with me," he replied. "I didn't say anything about rest."

# THIRTY-TWO

Clint and Marthayn went back to her tent, and as soon as they were inside she turned to him and they embraced and kissed.

"You're supposed to rest," she said breathlessly.

"Fletcher said something about resting," Clint said, "not me."

He pulled her to him and kissed her again. Her mouth was soft and tasty—although he couldn't have said what it tasted like. He guessed it tasted like her, so it was unlike anything he had ever tasted before.

He went on tasting it for a long time.

The cot Marthayn slept on was not big enough for both of them so she used some blankets to make a bed for them on the floor. To do this they had to move the table with the crystal ball from the center of the tent.

He undressed first as she watched, and then he settled down onto the bed of blankets and watched her.

"It should be darker in here," she said.

"Why?"

She hesitated, then said, "You embarrass me."

"How?"

"By watching me," she said. "I've never had anyone watch me the way you do."

"I don't want to miss anything," he said.

She put her hands to her face and said, "See, you embarrass me, even when you speak."

He could see that she was sincere, because her face had flushed pink.

"I'm only saying what comes to mind, Marthayn," he said. "You're beautiful, and I want to see you naked."

She stared at him, her arms folded in front of her.

"Would you like me to undress you?" he asked.

"I—I don't know."

"Do you want me to leave?"

"No!" she said emphatically.

"All right . . ."

He stood up and moved to her. He was already erect, and her eyes were on him as he got closer. When he was in front of her, she dropped her hands to her sides. He palmed her full breasts through her blouse, then took hold of it at the bottom and pulled it up over her head gently. He removed her skirt and her frilly undergarments and in moments she was naked—and blushing again.

Her breasts were full and firm, her flesh pale and smooth. The nipples were a light pink, not much darker than the rest of her skin. She was full through the hips and thighs, which he liked. He also liked the fact that she had a belly and that her ribs were not starkly visible. Clint preferred women like this, full and soft, yet firm and strong and possessed of unbelievable sensual appeal.

He kissed her then, as if to put her at ease and make her forget her embarrassment. Apparently it worked because she lifted her hands from her sides and ran the tips of her fingers over his erect penis.

He kissed her for a long time, then moved his lips over her neck and shoulders. When his mouth touched the spot where her neck and shoulders met, she shivered, and he knew it was a sensitive place for her. He took advantage of that knowledge and bit her there. He ran his hands over her body and felt the gooseflesh his bite had caused.

"Oh, God," she said, "that's too good . . ."

She closed one hand over his penis and began to stroke it.

He kissed her neck again, and her shoulder, and then moved his mouth down to her breasts. As his lips touched her left nipple, he once again found her to be remarkably responsive.

She moaned and squeezed him as he tongued her nipples.

"Oh, God," she said again, "my legs are weak . . ."

"Let's lie down," he suggested.

They did so, moving to the blankets together. He gathered her into his arms and peppered her flesh with kisses and bites, sucking on her nipples until she was crying out so loud he was sure that people outside the tent could hear.

He didn't care, and he was sure she didn't either.

Very quickly Clint got caught up in not only the feel of Marthayn's flesh, but the smell of her. At that moment he thought she was the most fragrant, sweetest-tasting woman he had ever been with—and certainly one of the most responsive.

He continued to explore her flesh with his mouth and hands, and she continued to moan and clutch at him. At one point she dug her nails into him, but he barely noticed. Finally, he worked his way down to between her legs.

"Oooh, what are you going to . . ." she started to ask, but he cut her off by touching his tongue to her wet clitoris, and the response was almost as if lightning had struck her.

He continued to work on her with his mouth and tongue, sliding his hands beneath her to cup her buttocks while he pleasured her.

Clint was feeling more alive than he had in months. Marthayn had responded to the way he looked at her, the way he talked to her, and now she was reacting to every touch of his hands and his mouth like no other woman ever had.

And later, he'd find out that she could dish it out as well as take it.

For now, though, as he continued to revel in the taste of her, she suddenly shuddered and cried out and it was as if she had lost control of her limbs. Her orgasm was one of the most intense he'd ever seen, and he'd seen a lot of women have orgasms. Even after he removed his mouth from her and moved up next to her to hold her, the spasms seemed to go on and on and on. . . .

# THIRTY-THREE

"I didn't think you were ever going to stop coming."

Marthayn did not move, content to lie with Clint's arms around her.

"Neither did I," she confided. "I've never felt anything like that before in my life."

"I like that."

"What?"

"That you'd admit that."

"Why not?" she asked. "It's the truth."

"Well, I'll tell you something that's true, then," he said.

"What?"

He reached across her belly and down between her legs and said, "You may be the wettest woman I've ever met."

"Oh, God," she said, hiding her face in his shoulder, "I know. I can't help it. It just . . . happens."

"Well," he said, moving his hand a bit, "it doesn't just happen."

"Well, no," she said, pressing her thighs tightly around his hand, "it doesn't. You had something to do with it."

"I had a lot to do with it."

Her hand strayed down between his legs where she stroked his semierect penis. Immediately it started to swell.

"You mean like I have something to do with this?" she asked.

She ran her fingers along the underside of his penis and his hips twitched.

"Oh," she said, "you like that, huh?"

"Oh, yes . . ."

She turned and slithered down his body until she was covering his crotch with kisses. She never touched his penis, but worked all around it, kissing his thighs, his belly, his hips, and then she went further down, over his legs until she was down by his feet.

"What are you doing down there?" he asked.

"Just relax," she said, touching his feet with her mouth.

He did as she commanded and felt her tongue moving over his toes, first the small one, then the next, and the next, and finally when she reached the big toe she took it fully into her mouth and sucked wetly.

"Oh, Jesus . . ." he said, as the feeling seemed to go from his toe right to his crotch.

She bit his toe then and moved on to the other foot. She spent a long time on it, finishing by licking his arch, which made him pull his foot away.

"Ticklish?"

"No," he said, "I just don't like it."

"Oh?" She licked his ankle. "Do you like this?"

"Yes."

Another lick, higher.

"And this?"

"Yes."

Higher still.

"And that?"

"Yes."

She ran her tongue up along the inside of his thigh, looking at him the whole time.

"And that?"

"Oh, yes."

She moved her tongue higher until she was licking the base of his penis and his testicles.

"Oh," he said, before she could ask, "yes . . ."

She ran the tip of her tongue along the underside of his penis until she reached the head, which she kissed gently before sucking on it. She took it into her mouth and began to move on him, sucking up and down, working it deeper and deeper, sliding her hand beneath him and sliding her fingers along his testicles and underneath to his buttocks.

She continued to suck him more and more avidly until he felt the rush building in his legs, rumbling through him. He could tell that this was going to be one of those rare eruptions, the kind that felt so good they almost hurt.

And he was right. . . .

# THIRTY-FOUR

In his wagon Matthew was sitting in the dark thinking about what he had seen that afternoon. He'd watched Clint Adams hit everything that Marthayn had held or thrown in the air. He was impressed by the man's marksmanship, but he still did not see how the man was a threat to him. He didn't doubt for a moment that Fletcher had brought the Gunsmith in to get rid of him somehow, but he just didn't feel threatened by the man.

There was a knock on the door of his wagon.

"Who is it?"

There was no answer.

That told him who it was.

He went to the door and opened it. Frank Flora stood there.

"What is it, Frank?" he asked. "I don't remember sending for you."

Frank Flora stared at Matthew, then touched his right hand to his hip.

"What's that supposed to mean, a gun? Oh, you mean the Gunsmith?"

Frank nodded.

"You think he's going to be a problem?"

Frank nodded again.

"Don't worry, he's not going to be a problem," Matthew said.

Frank lifted a hand to gesture, but Matthew stopped him.

"Look," Matthew said, "the sheriff can be more of a problem to us than Clint Adams. You've got to get your brother to pull up stakes. We have to move out of here tomorrow, before the sheriff decides to do something. Do you understand?"

Frank nodded.

"Is the money safe?"

Another nod.

"Good, Frank, good," Matthew said. "After today's performance you talk to your brother— or do whatever it is you and him do. Okay?"

Frank nodded.

"Now get away from here before someone sees you," Matthew said, and closed his door.

# THIRTY-FIVE

Clint fired and hit the ace of spades Marthayn was holding dead center. It barely moved in her hand. She walked toward the crowd and held the card so they could all see that it had been pierced right where the spade was. They oohed and aahed because Clint Adams had hit everything he had shot at.

The ace of the spades was the finale of the show, except for the part about shooting with the Gunsmith.

"All right, ladies and gentlemen," Fletcher Flora called out, "it's that time. Who among you would like to pit your skills with a gun against those of the Gunsmith?"

No one came forward.

"Come, come, ladies and gentlemen, surely there's someone among you who can shoot."

Clint watched the crowd, and he didn't see any takers among them.

Fletcher looked at Clint, a helpless expression on his face.

"Maybe they'd like to see somebody else shoot against me first, Fletch," Clint said.

"Like who?"

"Like maybe you."

Fletcher laughed and shook his head.

"I've never fired a gun in my life," Fletcher announced to everyone.

"Maybe you'll get lucky," Clint said.

Fletcher laughed again.

"I doubt it."

Clint was about to say something else when the sound of horses attracted the attention of everyone.

"What the hell—" Fletcher said.

Clint moved alongside him and said, "It's the sheriff and his deputies."

"Oh, God," the carny boss said, "not now."

"Show's over, Fletch," Clint said. "Announce it."

Clint left him making the announcement and walked over to intercept Sheriff Goodman and three of his deputies.

"You missed the show, Sheriff," Clint said.

"That so?" Goodman asked. "I didn't know you was part of it, Adams."

"Just for today," Clint said.

"Well, that's good," Goodman said, "because there ain't gonna be no show tomorrow."

"Is that so?" Clint asked. "Why?"

"Because everybody in town is clean, Adams," Goodman said. "I'm betting the bank robbers are out here, and I'm gonna find them."

Clint turned around and saw a big crowd of people coming toward them. He, the sheriff, and his deputies were standing between the people and their transportation, their horses and wagons that they'd used to come out here from the surrounding county. Most of the folks who lived in Benton's Fork were too upset about the bank robbery and too suspicious of the carnival to patronize it today.

"I think you're going to have to wait for the crowd to thin out before you start questioning the carnies, Sheriff," Clint said.

"Carnies?"

"That's what they call themselves," Clint explained.

"Well, most likely one or more of these carnies robbed our bank, Adams," Sheriff Goodman said. "I hope you don't mind if I try to find out who it was, and if the money's anywhere around here?"

"Why would I mind, Sheriff?" Clint said. "You're just doing your job."

The sheriff frowned.

"You won't try to interfere?"

"Why would I?"

They were being jostled now by the people moving past them.

"That was great shooting, Mr. Adams," someone said to Clint, and then others commented as they went by him.

A small boy going past tugged on his arm and said, "You shoot like magic, mister."

"There's nothing magic about it, son."

"Could I learn to shoot like that?"

"Probably," Clint said.

But before the boy could ask anything else his mother hurried him away.

"Sheriff," Clint said, "I'll talk to you later."

"Hey—" Goodman said, but Clint had already plunged into the crowd.

He worked his way through the swarm of people leaving the grounds until he was past them.

"What's going on?" Marthayn asked when she saw him.

"The sheriff is convinced that the bank was robbed by one of your people."

"That's silly."

"Is it?" Clint asked. "Do you know that for a fact, Marthayn?"

She opened her mouth to answer, then hesitated.

"You don't, do you?"

"Not for a fact," she said. "How could I?"

"Right, how could you," Clint said.

"All I know is *I* had nothing to do with it. What are the sheriff and his men going to do?"

"Search," Clint said, "and question."

"Where?" she asked. "Who?"

"Everywhere," he said, "and everyone."

"We'd better tell Fletch," she said.

"He probably knows," Clint said, "but let's go tell him."

# THIRTY-SIX

Clint and Marthayn found Fletcher surrounded by many of his people and listened to what he had to say.

"Whatever happens I want you all to cooperate with the sheriff and his men," he said. "Answer whatever questions they have, and give them access to your quarters. Is that understood?"

Everyone either nodded or said that it was.

Fletcher turned away from them and saw Clint and Marthayn watching him.

"Did you hear that?"

Clint wasn't sure if the man was asking him, Marthayn, or both of them, so he nodded and allowed Marthayn to answer out loud.

"I heard it," she said. "I have nothing to hide, Fletch."

"Good."

"Do you?" Clint asked.

Fletcher turned and looked at him.

"Marthayn," he said, without looking at her, "see if you can find Frank, will you?"

"What about Matthew?" she asked. "Is he going to cooperate?"

"I'll talk to Matthew," he said. "Go on, find my brother."

She looked at Clint, who nodded to her, and she left them alone.

"What makes you think I have something to hide?" Fletcher asked.

"I didn't say I thought that," Clint said. "I asked you if you did."

"I have nothing to hide, Clint," he said. "I don't know anything about the bank robbery."

"And how sure are you about your people?"

"My people are innocent," Fletcher said.

"Does that include Matthew?"

"I'll let him speak for himself."

Clint turned and saw the sheriff and his deputies approaching. Sheriff Goodman had a very determined look on his face.

"I guess he'll have to."

Matthew knew what was going on. He had watched Clint's act from his wagon and had observed the arrival of the sheriff and his men. He knew he was going to have to suffer the questions of the lawman. The sheriff could search to his heart's content and he wouldn't find anything in Matthew's wagon.

The magician wondered where Frank was at that moment.

Frank Flora was panicky. It was easy to make people think that he never felt any emotion. Emotion was very often detected in the tone of a man's voice, but since he couldn't talk he did not betray himself that way. Now, however, he was feeling panic inside as the sheriff and his men began to search and question. He didn't know what to do. He was sure that if anybody could see how scared he was, it would be his brother. But Fletcher would cover for him; he was sure of that. Fletcher was always there for him, covering for him, helping him . . . and telling him what to do.

Always telling him what to do. Well, maybe it was time for Fletcher to find out that Frank wasn't just the dutiful and silent brother. Maybe it was time for the older brother to find out that the younger brother could think for himself.

All he had to do now was control the fear that was forming in his stomach like ice.

# THIRTY-SEVEN

Fletcher Flora stayed with Sheriff Goodman, who was doing a wagon by wagon search for the stolen money. The three deputies were going around questioning the carnies about their whereabouts the night of the robbery. Clint wandered around the area, watching the activity because he wasn't directly involved in any of it. Actually, he was waiting for the sheriff to get to Matthew's wagon. That he wanted to see.

Marthayn had not been able to locate Frank Flora, which Clint found odd. Although Frank wasn't always in sight, Clint figured the man was always around the carnival grounds. Frank was an enigma to Clint, possibly because he was always silent. You could learn so much from a man's tone of voice, even more so than from a facial expression. Clint felt that a tone of voice was more difficult to control than an expression was. That was what made Frank Flora such a mystery. There was no way to tell what the man was really thinking.

Marthayn came up next to Clint and said, "They're not going to find anything."

He looked at her.

"Still haven't found Frank?"

"No."

"Does he have his own wagon?"

"Yes."

"Has it been searched yet?"

"No," she said. "If Fletch can't find Frank, though, he said he'd let the sheriff into the wagon."

"What do you think of Frank, Marthayn?"

She didn't answer right away.

"He's strange," she finally said.

"How?"

"Well, he seems to be very loyal to Fletch, but . . ." She let her voice trail off.

"But what?"

She shook her head and said, "I just get the feeling there's more going on than we know inside of Frank."

"Like what?"

She hesitated again.

"Where are you drawing these opinions from, Marthayn? Woman's intuition, or some clairvoyant power?"

"I think we both know I have no clairvoyant power," she said.

"What was that business of me meeting a tall, dark man?" he asked.

"Oh, that. Fletch told me to tell you that, so when you met Matthew you'd think it was true. I told him you wouldn't believe it, but . . ."

"Walk me over to Frank's wagon," Clint said. "I want to hear everything you know about Frank and Matthew."

"Why?"

"Because they're the two people I know the least about," he said, "and the two I want to know the most about."

She shrugged and said, "I'll tell you what I know."

Marthayn confided to Clint that she had not actually seen Matthew in months. Every time she went to his wagon he kept it dark inside. She could feel him, and smell him—but for the smell, she said, and his voice, he could have been a different man each time.

"You had sex with him," Clint said.

"Yes," she said, "but there was very little enjoyment in it for me. He took his pleasure, and then I left. Most men are like that, Clint."

"Really?"

She grinned shyly and said, "Present company excepted, of course."

"Why thank you."

"Come on, Clint," she said, "you've had women tell you before that you're unlike other men."

"I don't think I want to talk about that right now, Marthayn."

"Why not?"

"Because we'll end up back in your tent."

"Would that be so bad?"

"No," he said, "but let's save that for later. Keep telling me about Matthew."

"There's nothing else to tell. I always knew it was him, even in the dark."

"Do you know his last name?"

"Oh, no, he never told me."

"Does Fletch know?"

"I doubt it."

"He must have one."

"Maybe he does," she said, "but since I've know him he's just been the Great Matthew."

They reached a wagon and Marthayn said, "This is Frank's."

It was similar to all the other wagons in the camp, the writing on the side proclaiming it to be part of the CARNIVAL FLORA.

"The door's locked?"

"I don't know," she said. "I didn't try it."

"Well," he said, looking around, "let's give it a try."

# THIRTY-EIGHT

Clint moved to the wagon and mounted the three wooden steps that led up to the door. Marthayn looked around nervously as Clint tried the door and found it open.

"I'm going inside," he told her. "Let me know if you see anyone."

"Clint, wait—" she said, but he went in without listening.

Inside he found it dark and looked around for a lamp. By the light coming in from the door he found one and lit it, then closed the door behind him.

The inside of the wagon was a mess. Clothing and bedding were all over the place. Clint wondered if Frank was involved in the robbery of the bank, if he'd be foolish enough to keep the money here, in his own wagon.

He began to look around, taking no care because the place was a mess anyway. All the while he listened for Marthayn's warning that someone was coming, either the Sheriff or Frank himself.

He didn't find anything until he looked underneath Frank's pallet. There was no money, but there was something that felt like burlap, and when he pulled it out it turned out to be a money bag, the kind used in banks. Only it didn't say BANK OF BENTON'S FORK, ARIZONA, it said BANK OF SURREY, COLORADO.

"Jesus," he said aloud. If Frank hadn't robbed the Benton's Fork bank, he certainly had had something to do with another bank robbery. Were there others as well?

Shaking his head, Clint tried to decide what to do. If he took the bag with him, then the sheriff wouldn't find it, but why did he owe that to Frank Flora? If the man was guilty, he deserved to be caught and punished, right?

Finally, he decided to put the bag back where he'd gotten it. He searched a little more and the only thing he found of interest was an old Navy Colt. He checked it and found it loaded and in working condition, and put it back where he got it.

The only other thing he found was a spare pair of boots worn down on the outsides of the heels, indicating that Frank walked that way, coming down on the outsides of the heels first and hardest.

Satisfied that there was nothing else of inter-

est in the wagon, he left and found Marthayn
fidgeting nervously outside.

"It's about time," she said. "Did you find anything?"

"Let's go someplace else," he said, taking her
arm, "and talk about it."

# THIRTY-NINE

"What did you find?"

They were in her tent, and she had prepared a cup of tea. She told him that Fletcher would save her tent for last and wouldn't bring the sheriff around until he was done everyplace else.

Clint told her about the canvas bank bag he'd found under Frank's bed.

"Then he did rob the bank?"

"Not necessarily," Clint said. "He probably had something to do with robbing another bank. If that's the case, then there's a good chance he had something to do with robbing this one."

"You're confusing me."

"There's no proof he robbed the bank in Benton's Fork," Clint said, "but the bag will probably be enough for the sheriff to hold him."

"What did you do with the bag?"

"I left it where I found it."

"So the sheriff's going to find it."

"Right."

"And arrest him."

"Probably."

"What if Frank doesn't know it's there?"

"You mean somebody else put it there to frame him?" he asked.

She nodded.

"Like who?"

"Like Matthew."

"Everybody wants Matthew to be guilty so the sheriff will take him away. Why doesn't Fletcher just face him and tell him to leave?"

"I suppose he's afraid."

"Because he believes in Matthew's magic?" Clint asked. "That's ridiculous."

"When you've lived among . . . unusual people for as long as Fletch has, Clint," she said, "you have an . . . open mind about a lot of things."

"Let's get over to Matthew's wagon," Clint said, "before the sheriff searches it."

"He may already have," she said, as Clint moved to the tent flap.

"Then let's hurry!"

# FORTY

When Clint and Marthayn reached Matthew's wagon, there was no one around. On the way they had passed some of the deputies talking to the Carnies, but they hadn't seen the sheriff and Fletcher Flora.

"Maybe they've been here and gone," she said.

"I don't think so," Clint said, looking at the ground. "It looks like there's only been one person here in the past few hours."

"How can you tell?"

He knelt down and said, "These tracks are a few hours old." He pointed to footprints that showed boots that were worn down on the outsides of the heels. "It was Frank."

"What?" she asked, in disbelief. "How can you know that?"

"Look at these heel prints," Clint said. "I found a pair of boots in Frank's wagon that had heels just like this."

"What was Frank doing here?" she asked.

"Haven't you ever seen him talking to Matthew?" Clint asked, standing up.

"No," she said. They both knew that "talking to" was the wrong phrase, but neither said anything. "Fletcher's the only one I've ever seen with him."

"Well, I guess Matthew and Frank have been, uh, communicating behind Fletcher's back."

Clint looked at the wagon and wondered if Matthew was watching them, even now.

"Clint?"

"Yeah?"

"The sheriff's coming with Fletch."

Clint turned and saw the two men approaching.

"What are you doing here?" Goodman asked.

"Waiting for you."

"Why?"

"This is going to be interesting," Clint said. He looked at Fletcher and asked, "Did you find anything anywhere else?"

"No," Fletcher said.

"What's left?"

"Here," Fletcher said, "Marthayn's tent, Frank's wagon, and mine."

"How are you going to get into Matthew's wagon?" Clint asked.

Fletcher looked at Sheriff Goodman and said, "That's his problem."

Clint watched as Goodman approached the wagon and banged on the door.

"Open up," he shouted. "It's the law."

There was no answer.

"Hey!" Goodman pounded again.

When there was no answer he turned and asked Fletcher, "Is he in there?"

"Oh," Fletcher said, "he's in there."

"What makes you so sure?"

"The only time he leaves the wagon is to do his act," Fletcher said. "He's in there."

"Well, make him come out."

"I can't make him come out."

"He works for you, doesn't he? You're his boss, ain't you? Make him open the door."

"I can't make him do anything he doesn't want to do. You want him out, you'll have to make him come out yourself."

The sheriff turned back to the door and banged his fist on it.

"I know you're in there, Matthew," he called out. "If you don't come out, I'm gonna break this door down. This is the law, damn it."

They all waited to see if the door would open. Goodman took out his gun, indicating that he was prepared to shoot the lock to get the door open. Actually, the wooden door of the wagon was flimsy enough simply to be kicked in. If he fired through the door, he'd probably hit Matthew and kill him.

"Don't shoot, Goodman," Clint said. He looked at Fletcher and asked, "Is he going to come out?"

Abruptly Fletcher looked at the sky and said, "It's the right time of day. The sun's going down. He'll come out, all right."

With that Clint heard the click of the lock and the door began to open very slowly.

Sheriff Goodman backed away a few feet, keeping his gun ready.

Marthayn leaned forward a little out of curiosity.

Fletcher, who was the only person who was supposed to have seen Matthew out of costume of late, looked excited. Maybe, Clint thought, he was hoping that the sheriff would shoot Matthew as soon as he came out.

As for Clint, he kept his eyes on the door, waiting for Matthew to make his grand appearance. He had seen the man during his act, in full regalia with black suit and black cape with red lining.

He wondered what the man would be wearing now.

# FORTY-ONE

The magician stepped into the doorway and looked out at the foursome. He was dressed as if he were going to put on a performance—and maybe he was.

"Fletcher," he said.

"Hello, Matthew."

"What's all the commotion about?"

Fletcher pointed to the lawman.

"The sheriff is questioning everyone and searching everyone's quarters," he said.

"For what?"

"Money," Goodman said coldly.

"I don't have much money," Matthew said. "Fletcher here doesn't pay me very much."

Clint was studying Matthew. Aside from the fact that he was tall and dark and looked good dressed in black, he appeared fairly ordinary.

"Not your money," Goodman said, "the town's money, money that was stolen from the bank."

"Oh," Matthew said, "I heard about that. Your bank was robbed."

"That's right."

"How much?" Matthew asked.

"Close to forty thousand dollars," Sheriff Goodman said.

Clint was watching Matthew at that moment and saw something pass over his face.

"Forty thousand," the magician said. "That's a lot of money."

"Do you know anything about it?"

"Oh, no," Matthew said, "I can truthfully say I don't know anything about forty thousand dollars."

Goodman gestured at the magician's wagon.

"I want to go in there and have a look."

Matthew turned and looked at his wagon, then turned back to the sheriff.

"In there?"

"That's right."

"There's no money in there."

"Isn't there?"

"No."

"Well," Goodman said, "I'll want to have a look anyway."

"I don't think I can let you do that, Sheriff."

"And why not?"

"Well, there are a lot of things in that wagon that no one is meant to see but me."

The sheriff got a surprised look on his face, like he thought Matthew was about to confess.

"Like what?"

"Secrets."

"What kind of secrets?"

"Oh, secrets of my trade, Sheriff," Matthew said. "Magician's secrets."

Matthew finally came down the steps and approached the sheriff. He put his hand out to the man and suddenly there was a flash of light from his palm.

Sheriff Goodman staggered back a few steps and waved his hand in front of him, as if warding off the flash.

Marthayn caught her breath just in time to keep from screaming.

Fletcher showed no sign of surprise.

Clint started, but averted his eyes quickly enough to miss being blinded.

"Secrets," Matthew said, showing the sheriff his clean palm, "like how I did that, and other things. See, I don't let anyone into my wagon, Sheriff . . . not anyone."

# FORTY-TWO

"I'm afraid I'm gonna have to insist, mister," Goodman said. "Now step aside."

Abruptly, Matthew turned and waved his arm at the wagon. In response—or seemingly so—the door slammed.

"What the—" Goodman said, and ran to the door. He tried it, but it was locked. "How did you do that?" the lawman demanded.

"Magic," Matthew said, waving his hand.

Goodman took out his gun.

"Open it now or I shoot the door open."

"Go ahead," Matthew said, "but I won't be responsible for what happens."

Goodman frowned and asked, "What could happen?"

"All I'm saying," Matthew said, "is that I

won't be responsible for your death."

"My . . . death?" Goodman scowled, not sure whether he was being threatened or not.

Suddenly one of the deputies called out from a few yards away. "Sheriff Goodman, come quick! We found something in one of the wagons!"

The sheriff stared hard at Matthew. "You stay right here, mister, or I'll come after you with a posse."

Matthew looked unimpressed. Goodman hurried off with a concerned Fletcher following him.

"Clint, they're heading toward Frank's wagon," Marthayn said.

"Maybe they found the bank bag from Surrey," Clint said.

"Surrey?" Marthayn paled. "You didn't tell me it was from Surrey."

"Did you play Surrey?" he asked her.

"Yes," Marthayn said, "after Matthew joined us."

Clint whirled on Matthew.

"So you robbed that bank too."

"I what?"

"You and Frank Flora."

Matthew stared at Clint for a few moments before replying.

"Would it do any good to tell you that you're crazy?" he asked.

"No."

Matthew pulled at the string of his cape. "You can't prove anything."

"Frank has a burlap bag from Surrey in his

wagon," Clint said. "Your doing?"

Matthew didn't answer.

"It wasn't very smart, Matthew," Clint said. "When the sheriff arrests Frank, he'll give you to the law."

"I have to go back inside," Matthew said.

"The sheriff will be back," Marthayn said.

"No," Matthew said, "I don't think so."

She looked at Clint.

"Goodman may just settle for Frank," he told her. "He might not look any further."

Matthew smiled and headed for the wagon.

"You made one mistake, didn't you, Matthew?" Clint called out.

Matthew turned.

"You believed Frank when he told you how much money he got out of the Benton's Fork bank," Clint said.

The magician did not reply.

"When the sheriff said that forty thousand dollars was taken from the bank, you were surprised. What did Frank tell you? Ten? Twenty?"

Matthew remained silent.

"If he's arrested, how will you find the rest of the money?" Clint asked.

Matthew turned and walked to his wagon.

"Or do you even know where any of the money is?"

The magician went up the steps and opened the door by hand.

As the door was closing behind him, Clint called out, "How come you didn't open it without touching it?"

# FORTY-THREE

Clint and Marthayn hurried to Frank's wagon. As they reached the wagon, the sheriff was coming out, carrying the burlap bag.

"Do you know what this is?" Goodman asked Clint.

"No," Clint lied, "what?"

"It's a bag from a bank," Goodman said, holding it high, "a bank in Surrey, Colorado, that was robbed last month." Goodman turned and waved the bag at Fletcher. "In your brother's wagon!"

Fletcher looked stunned.

"It's not possible," he said. "Frank wouldn't do that—"

"This is all the proof I need," Goodman said. "He did the bank in Surrey, and probably our bank too. Where is he?"

"I—I don't know," Fletcher said. "He should be around here—"

"Well, if he is, my men and I will find him," Goodman said. "If you try to warn him, I'll take you in too. Understand?"

The lawman didn't wait for an answer. He turned and nodded to his deputy to follow.

"I don't understand . . ." Fletcher said helplessly.

"It's Matthew, Fletch," Marthayn said.

"What?"

"Matthew put the bag in Frank's wagon."

"How do you know?"

"Clint figured it out."

Fletcher looked at him.

"You knew that bag was there?"

"Yes."

"And you left it there?"

"At the time I didn't think it was planted," Clint said. "Besides, your brother *is* guilty of bank robbery, Fletch."

"I don't understand."

"Matthew and Frank have been robbing banks, probably in certain towns you've played near."

"If they've been working together, why would Matthew hide that bag in his wagon?"

"To throw suspicion off himself in case a search was ever made—like today."

"Why didn't you tell the sheriff?"

"Because I can't prove Matthew is involved," Clint said. "Only Frank can do that."

"How?"

"We've got to find him before the law does and get him to turn himself in—and give Matthew up."

"But . . . he'll go to jail."

"He's going to go to jail anyway, Fletcher," Clint said. "Why leave Matthew outside, free as a bird?"

"I don't know . . ." Fletcher said, shaking his head.

"Fletch," Clint said, "if we don't find him first, the sheriff and his men might kill him. You don't want that, do you?"

"No!"

"Then where is he?"

"I don't know."

"Well," Clint said, "he's your brother, Fletch. You're just going to have to figure out where he might hide."

"You don't understand," Fletcher said. "Frank wouldn't know where to hide unless I told him. He can't think for himself."

"You know, Fletch," Clint said, "I think you're guilty of underestimating your brother just because he's mute."

Fletcher thought a moment and then said with a look of wonder on his face, "I guess you're right, Clint."

"So you tell me, Fletch," Clint said. "What do we do now?"

For the first time since Clint had met him, Fletcher looked truly frightened. There had been a hint of it once or twice when he talked about Matthew, but now it was stark.

"I don't know, Clint," he said, wringing his large hands, "I don't know."

"All right, then," Clint said. "I'll tell you what to do. Get your people out looking for Frank. If they find him, they call for you and me, no one else—and they don't try to talk to him themselves."

"Nobody talks to Frank, anyway," Fletcher said absently.

"Good," Clint said, "let's keep it that way."

"We've got to keep Frank out of jail, Clint," Fletcher said. "We've got to. He's my brother."

"I'm afraid we can only do that if we can turn Matthew in, with the money. That's going to mean standing up to him, Fletch."

"Standing up to Matthew," Fletcher repeated.

"That's right."

Fletcher rubbed his hand over his face.

"Let's find Frank first, though," Clint said. "Go ahead, get a move on."

Fletcher nodded and left Marthayn and Clint standing there.

"What are you thinking?" she asked.

"You can't tell?"

She shook her head.

"I only know that something's on your mind."

"It's what Fletch said about keeping Frank out of jail," Clint said.

"What about it?"

"What if it's Frank who's running Matthew," Clint said, "and not the other way around?"

# FORTY-FOUR

The sheriff and his deputies searched the entire camp for Frank. So did the carnies, led by Fletcher.

After that the lawmen started to search outside the camp. Fletcher and the carnies did the same for a while, but then they stopped.

"He wouldn't go too far from the camp," Fletcher said. "I know that."

"Even on the run?" Clint asked.

"Even then," the man said. "I know my brother."

"You didn't know that he was robbing banks," Clint reminded him.

Fletcher pointed a finger at Clint and said angrily, "I still don't! I won't know that until I look into my brother's eyes."

The sheriff and his men kept widening the area of their search until they were far enough away from the camp that Clint could no longer hear them. Fletcher and his carnies had given up.

"I might know where he is," Clint said suddenly.

"What?" Marthayn said.

"Where?" Fletcher asked.

"Come with me."

"In there?" Fletcher asked. They were standing outside the magician's wagon. "With Matthew?"

"It's the only place the sheriff hasn't looked, remember?" Clint asked.

"How do we get in?" Marthayn asked.

"We knock," Clint said. "Matthew will come out."

"He's already come out once today," Marthayn reminded him.

"He'll come out again."

"How can you be so sure?"

"Because," Clint said, "he doesn't want us to go in."

Fletcher and Marthayn waited while Clint went to the wagon and knocked on the door.

"Go away."

"Open up, Matthew. It's Clint Adams, and Fletcher Flora."

"I said, go away."

"Come on," Clint said, "we want Frank."

"He's not here."

"We know he's in there."

There was a moment's hesitation and then Matthew asked, "What makes you think that?"

"Because he's not anywhere out here, Matthew," Clint said. He banged on the door again. "Come on, open up or I'll shoot through the door."

"You wouldn't."

"Try me."

Clint waited a moment and then the lock on the door clicked. He backed away as the door opened. Fletcher moved forward to stand next to him. Marthayn stayed in the background.

Matthew appeared in the doorway, still dressed in his costume. Clint now wondered if he dressed that way all the time.

"You're taking a big chance bothering me, Adams," Matthew said.

"Look, friend," Clint said, "unlike everyone else around here I don't happen to think you have any magical powers, so don't try to scare me."

"I don't scare you, huh?"

"No," Clint said.

They stared at each other.

"Where's my brother, Matthew?" Fletcher demanded.

"I wouldn't know, Fletcher," Matthew said. "You keep better track of him than I do."

"I don't think that's true," Clint said. "I think you keep very close track of Frank—or he does of you."

"What's that mean?"

"I'm wondering, Matthew," Clint said, "who the brains of these bank robberies really was, you or Frank? Nobody sees you except when you do your act. It wouldn't be hard for you to step out, sneak into town, and open the safe. In fact, you're the magician, you're the one with the light fingers, you're probably the one who opens the safes."

"You must be joking," Matthew said. "Frank couldn't form a whole thought without me or his brother."

"So you say," Clint said.

"Ask his brother."

Clint looked at Fletcher, who nodded.

"I'm afraid he's right."

"So you're saying you were the brains and he opened the safes?"

"That's right," Matthew said. "It takes brains to plan—"

Suddenly the magician stopped, realizing he'd been tricked.

"You're a clever man, Adams."

"How did you get Frank to open the safes?"

"His brother might not know this, but the dummy is actually good with his hands. It started out with me teaching him some tricks, and then progressed to the safes. Of course, there were a few stops in between, but they're not important."

"You mean, it's true?" Fletcher asked. "You and my brother robbed those banks?"

"Sure, it's true," Matthew said.

"I'll tell the sheriff," Fletcher said.

"Who's going to believe you, Fletch? You're Frank's brother, you'd lie to protect him."

"What about me?" Clint asked.

"And me?" Marthayn called out.

Matthew's head jerked up when he heard her voice. He obviously hadn't seen her. His vision wasn't good in the light.

"Too many witnesses, Matthew," Clint said.

"Apparently," Matthew said. "Tell me, Adams, have you ever seen this one?"

Matthew's hand came up, there was a flash of light, and suddenly he was holding a gun on them.

# FORTY-FIVE

"Jesus!" Fletcher said. Marthayn gasped.

"That's pretty good," Clint said.

"Thank you."

"Tell me, when you make a gun appear like that, does it come with bullets?"

"Oh, yes, it's fully loaded," Matthew said, "except for one shot."

"One shot?"

"Yes," Matthew said, "you were right about Frank. He is inside."

"Frank!" Fletcher called.

"He can't hear you," Matthew said.

"You saying you shot him?" Fletcher asked. "We didn't hear a shot."

"My wagon is specially equipped, remember, Fletch? Nobody can hear what goes on inside . . . unless I want them to."

Clint didn't get that. They'd heard Matthew call out from inside; how could he fire a gun without the shot being heard?

"Jesus, you killed him? Why?"

"You tell him, Adams," Matthew said. "You figured it out."

"Frank lied about how much money he got out of the Benton's Fork bank," Clint said. "He got forty, but he told Matthew he got . . . how much?"

"Ten, the weasel," Matthew said. "Tried to hold out on me. After you left he came by, wanting a place to hide. I gave it to him."

"And shot him."

"After he revealed where the money was."

"How do you know he didn't lie?"

"Jesus, I hope he didn't."

"Why did you shoot him before checking?" Clint asked.

"Well, actually it was an accident. He went for the gun, and we struggled. It was right between us when it went off, which served to muffle the shot. Could have been me easily enough."

"So you killed him by accident," Clint said.

"I said that, didn't I?"

"But can you kill a man deliberately, while he's facing you?"

"And a woman?" Marthayn asked.

"And another man!" Fletcher said, fists clenched in grief and rage.

Matthew smiled, and Clint didn't like it one bit.

"I don't have much of a choice, do I?"

"The sheriff and his men are in the area," Marthayn said. "How are you going to explain our bodies?"

"Simple," Matthew said. "You found Frank here, he and Adams shot it out. They killed each other, and you and Fletcher were caught in the cross fire."

"And you?" Clint asked.

"Me? I saw the whole thing from the safety of my wagon."

"No magic to get you out of this one, huh, Matthew?"

"Sorry, Adams," the magician said. "Just a gun. You should appreciate that, huh?"

"I have some magic for you," Clint said. He was about to try something he hadn't done too many times before—drawing on an already drawn gun.

"Really?"

"Yes, it's a farewell trick. Just watch my hand," Clint said, moving his left hand slightly, just enough to attract the man's attention.

"Which han—" Matthew was saying when Clint drew and fired in one incredible, swift, lifesaving motion.

# FORTY-SIX

Clint watched as Sheriff Goodman's deputies carried away the bodies of the Great Matthew—although now he was the Not-So-Great Matthew—and Frank Flora. Hurrying along behind them was Fletcher Flora, mourning the death of his brother and taking full blame.

"It's my fault," he told Clint with tears in his eyes. "I never treated him right."

It was a little late for that, but Clint didn't say anything.

He was standing with Marthayn and Sheriff Goodman now. Goodman was holding an empty bag in his hand that he had recovered from Matthew's wagon. BENTON'S FORK BANK was written on it.

"You didn't find the money?" Marthayn asked.

"No," Goodman said, casting a glare Clint's way. "If Adams hadn't killed the magician . . ."

"He had no choice," Marthayn interrupted him. "Matthew was going to kill us. I've never seen anything like it. Matthew was already holding his gun, and Clint drew and shot him before he could get off a shot."

"A little misdirection," Clint said, speaking of his "watch my hand" remark to Matthew. "As a professional he should never have fallen for that."

"Well, the money will turn up. It has to. We won't stop looking until we find it. It has to be around here somewhere."

Sheriff Goodman stalked off after his men, holding the bank bag in his hand as if it were some great trophy.

"Do you think he'll find it?" Marthayn asked.

"Who knows?" Clint said. "He's right. It has to be hidden around here somewhere. He probably won't let you all leave until he finds it."

"But you can leave," she observed.

"I intend to," he said. "I only stayed out of curiosity, first about the carnival in general, and then about Matthew."

Marthayn looked at Matthew's wagon, her head cocked to one side.

"I don't know how he did it," she said.

"Did what?" Clint asked.

She turned and looked at him.

"Held us all under his thumb that way."

"He was a strong-willed man," Clint said. "Plus he had a few tricks up his sleeve."

"Hmm," she said.

"What?"

"Well, some of those tricks looked—I mean, they seemed—"

"Like real magic?"

She nodded.

"A lot of people thought so."

She was eyeing the magician's wagon.

"I can read your mind," Clint said.

"Can you?"

"Yes."

"What am I thinking?"

"That you'd like to go inside his wagon and maybe find out how he did some of those tricks."

"Hmm," she said, "you're pretty good."

They both stood there a few moments, looking at the wagon speculatively.

"Clint?"

"Yes?"

"Do you have to leave right away, or do you still have some curiosity left?"

He looked at her and said, "Well, maybe just a little. Why don't you lead the way?"

Watch for

**DAKOTA GUNS**

156th novel in the exciting GUNSMITH series
from Jove

*Coming in December!*

# If you enjoyed this book, subscribe now and get...

# TWO FREE

## A $7.00 VALUE—

# J. R. ROBERTS

# THE GUNSMITH

Payable in U.S. funds. No cash orders accepted. Postage & handling: $1.75 for one book, 75¢ for each additional. Maximum postage $5.50. Prices, postage and handling charges may change without notice. Visa, Amex, MasterCard call 1-800-788-6262, ext. 1, refer to ad # 206d

Or, check above books    **Bill my:** ☐ Visa ☐ MasterCard ☐ Amex _____

and send this order form to:                           (expires)

The Berkley Publishing Group    Card#_____

390 Murray Hill Pkwy., Dept. B                         ($15 minimum)

East Rutherford, NJ 07073    Signature_____

Please allow 6 weeks for delivery.    **Or enclosed is my:** ☐ check ☐ money order

Name_____    Book Total    $_____

Address_____    Postage & Handling    $_____

City_____    Applicable Sales Tax $_____

                                   (NY, NJ, PA, CA, GST Can.)

State/ZIP_____    Total Amount Due    $_____

HARLEQUIN *Presents*

Don't forget Harlequin Presents EXTRA
now brings you a powerful new collection
every month featuring four books!

**Be sure not to miss any of the titles in**

# In the Greek Tycoon's Bed,

### available May 13:

## THE GREEK'S FORBIDDEN BRIDE
by Cathy Williams

## THE GREEK TYCOON'S UNEXPECTED WIFE
by Annie West

## THE GREEK TYCOON'S VIRGIN MISTRESS
by Chantelle Shaw

## THE GIANNAKIS BRIDE
by Catherine Spencer

## Coming Next Month

**Enjoy a gondola ride along the canals of Venice,
join a royal wedding party or take a romantic stroll through the
streets of London...all next month with Harlequin Romance®!**

### #4027 THE PREGNANCY PROMISE by Barbara McMahon
*Unexpectedly Expecting!*

What's on *your* wish list for the perfect guy? At the top of Lianne's is that
he will be a great father...to the child she longs for. In the first of this
heartwarming duet, Lianne's deepest desire may be fulfilled from the most
unexpected of places...by her gorgeous boss, Tray!

### #4028 THE ITALIAN'S CINDERELLA BRIDE by Lucy Gordon
*Heart to Heart*

A flash of lightning brings a young woman to Count Pietro Bagnelli's *palazzo*.
Though Pietro's turned against the world, he can't reject this bedraggled waif.
But can Ruth find a fairy-tale ending with the proud, damaged count?

### #4029 SOS MARRY ME! by Melissa McClone
*The Wedding Planners*

Only Mr. Right will do for wedding-dress designer Serena, and free-spirited
pilot Kane meets none of her criteria. Then he is forced to perform a crash
landing! Stranded with Serena, there's no denying the chemistry!

### #4030 HER ROYAL WEDDING WISH by Cara Colter
*By Royal Appointment*

Princess Shoshauna craves the freedom to marry for love, not duty. Then,
suddenly in danger, she is whisked to safety by unsuitable but daring soldier
Jake Ronan. She may owe him her life, but will she give him her hand...
in marriage?

### #4031 SAYING YES TO THE MILLIONAIRE by Fiona Harper
*A Bride for All Seasons*

Challenged by a friend, cautious Fern ends up on a four-day treasure hunt
with dreamy Josh Adams! Daredevil Josh never stays in one place—or with
one woman—for long. Could Fern be the exception to the rule?

### #4032 HER BABY, HIS PROPOSAL by Teresa Carpenter
*Baby on Board*

Navy SEAL Brock Sullivan's code of honor leads him to gallantly propose
to pregnant stranger Jesse, who needs his help and protection. But what
begins as a marriage of convenience starts to grow very complicated when
Brock comes home injured, needing loving care....

HRCNM0508